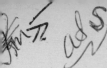

THE FASTEST MAN . . .

"You must have a reputation around town," Slocum said.

"You've heard of me? Billy Dee, the fastest man in New Mexico Territory."

"No, I just rode into town," Slocum said. The words hung like the miasma over a battlefield. He smelled blood and death.

"You're a fool," Dee said. Behind him came his three henchmen. Slocum noticed them but kept his attention on Billy Dee. The man was working himself up into a killing rage.

"How many you gunned down?" Slocum asked. "Two? Three?"

"I kilt nine! And you're gonna make number ten."

Billy Dee went for his six-gun. Two shots rang out. A smile came to Dee's face, then he crumpled to the ground. His six-shooter had discharged in his holster, never clearing leather when Slocum's slug had ripped out his foul heart.

"He was the fastest man I ever seen!" cried the scruffy henchman, staring at the corpse of his boss.

"He wasn't fast enough, not by half," Slocum said.

JAKE LOGAN

SLOCUM AND THE LAST GASP

J

JOVE BOOKS, NEW YORK

SLOCUM AND THE LAST GASP

A Jove Book / published by arrangement with
the author

PRINTING HISTORY
Jove edition / September 1998

The Penguin Putnam Inc. World Wide Web site address is
http://www.penguinputnam.com

ISBN: 0-515-12355-2

A JOVE BOOK®
Jove Books are published by The Berkley Publishing Group,
a member of Penguin Putnam Inc.,
200 Madison Avenue, New York, New York 10016.
JOVE and the "J" design are trademarks belonging to
Jove Publications, Inc.

PRINTED IN THE UNITED STATES OF AMERICA

10 9 8 7 6 5 4 3 2 1

SLOCUM AND THE LAST GASP

1

Jornada del Muerto. Journey of Death, the Spanish had called it, stretching from Mexico all the way up to Albuquerque. Slocum was riding it in the fall, when it was cooler. Still, getting through Tularosa and the badlands, complete with the peculiar desolate, burning-hot white sand stretching for endless miles, then finding a trail along the Rio Grande where he might retrieve a drop or two of water, would be quite a chore. Too much of one. So he crossed the mountains south of the Chupadera and followed a path north on the eastern slopes.

It was cooler riding in the fall. It was also drier. The rains had done little this year to put any water into the misnamed Rio Grande, and it might not be until spring runoff when there was enough to fill even a shot glass. But he found a few springs on the new route, more than he was likely to find along the *Jornada.*

Finally, Slocum brushed off the dust from his hat, wiped his forehead, and looked down Railroad Avenue. Albuquerque's White Elephant Saloon was a sight for sore eyes. Any place that sold whiskey would have been. He rode slowly down the street until he found a patch of shade where he could tether his horse.

"You done good," Slocum said, patting the horse's neck. He knew he ought to see to the animal before tending his own needs, but his throat was so dry he figured another ten minutes would be all it took to start raising cotton. Making sure the horse was near enough to the watering trough to slake some of its thirst, but not so much that it would bloat, Slocum went inside the cool dimness of the saloon.

He pulled out his pocket watch and studied it. Either it was running slow, or the saloon had a business to beat the band. It was only four in the afternoon and the place was packed.

"Come on in and join the fun," called the barkeep, a scrawny old galoot put together with toothpicks and a bit of spit to hold his bushy mustache in place.

"What's the cause for celebration?" Slocum asked, not caring. He pointed to a bottle of rotgut that didn't look too poisonous. Right now he was so thirsty he would have sucked the venom out of a rattler's fangs.

"Payday," the barkeep said, pouring a shot of the amber fluid. Slocum hesitated to call it whiskey, though the label declared it to be Billy Taylor's Finest. "Everyone flocks in here to spend their money real early on payday."

Slocum saw a big Regulator clock on the wall slowly ticking off the minutes, showing it to be just shy of seven o'clock. He checked his pocket watch again, and saw it had stopped. He gave the stem a few quick turns and got it running again. He heaved a sigh when he lifted it to his ear and heard its familiar tick-tick-ticking. The watch was all he had left to remind him of his brother Robert, save for sour memories of foolish, vainglorious generals and a war that should never have been fought.

"Mountains confused me as to the time. Been riding close to them on the other side and it gets dark sooner over there," Slocum said.

"You have the look of someone coming from Texas," the barkeep said. "You lookin' for . . . work?" The way he put it caused Slocum to turn cautious.

"Always looking for a decent job," he said carefully. "Mostly, I'm just passing through."

"To where?"

Slocum turned his piercing green eyes on the man, stared him down a mite, then said, "Haven't decided."

"Sorry, no offense, didn't mean nothin' by it," the barkeep said, moving away so fast his bones rattled like a skeleton's.

Slocum frowned as he drank, only part of it due to the acid bite of the liquor. He wasn't used to being questioned so closely when he came into a town, and certainly not by a bartender. Too many wanted posters floated throughout the West with his likeness on them. If a marshal had been doing the questioning, Slocum might have decided to move on then and there.

Dodging the law had been a problem ever since the war. He had ridden with Quantrill's Raiders and had done more than his share of killing, but when it came down to the August 21, 1863, raid on Lawrence, Kansas, where Quantrill had ordered every male over the age of eight slaughtered, Slocum had rebelled. He had done his share of killing, but not of children. That had got him gutshot by Bloody Bill Anderson and left for dead.

Months of recuperation finally let him make his way back to Slocum's Stand in Calhoun County, Georgia, property of the Slocum family since the time of George II. His parents were dead and his brother Robert had been killed at Little Roundtop. The spread was mighty lonely, but Slocum put his heart and soul into getting the place into decent shape. And he did, until a carpetbagger judge took a shine to the place.

Slocum had heard the judge wanted a place of his own to turn into a stud ranch, a place where Tennessee walkers could be raised. It turned out Slocum's Stand was that place. No taxes had been paid, claimed the judge. Slocum had no money. He barely had enough supplies to keep the farm working.

When the Reconstruction judge and his hired gunman rode out to take the farm, they found the real estate came with a heavy price. Slocum rode away that afternoon, two new graves on a hill. Ever since, his footsteps had been dogged with charges of judge-killing. Just about any crime could be forgotten except that one.

Slocum worried the barkeep might have recognized him. Too many of the men tending bar also worked as lawmen. Maybe this one had remembered a poster, had seen a picture that reminded him of Slocum. Without appearing to do so, Slocum reached over and slid the leather thong off the hammer of his Colt Navy. With the iron ready for action, Slocum reckoned he could take about any man in the room. Most of them looked to be cowboys and clerks and people who worked in Albuquerque at jobs less than high-paying.

He saw no one that might be a banker or even a business owner. That suited him just fine. These were workingmen who wanted nothing more than to keep their whistles wet with bad whiskey and forget their sorry lot in life for the duration of their drunk. No one was likely to put up much of a fuss unless the barkeep fetched the town marshal.

Slocum finished his drink and saw the barkeep wasn't likely to offer another any time soon. He leaned against the bar, studying the crowd. He found himself revising his original estimation of the clientele. At the back of the saloon, seated with three others at a green-felt-topped card table, was a well-dressed gent who had taken on a drink or two more than his capacity.

He was louder now and gambling carelessly. Slocum wished he had a few dollars to risk in a poker game.

This was the kind of well-heeled mark he enjoyed relieving of the burden of too many greenbacks.

"There a livery stable around here?" he called to the barkeep. The man pointed a thin finger in the direction of the setting sun. Slocum nodded and left, getting his horse away from the watering trough through the use of hard tugging and swats on its rump.

"You'll blow up if you drink any more," Slocum cautioned the still-thirsty horse. "How about a little hay to go along with those weeds you been eating?" Even the blue grama along the trail had been dry this year, giving little for the horse to eat. Slocum checked his pockets, found all the coins, and put together sixty-six cents, possibly enough for the horse's well-deserved meal.

He still had sixteen cents left when he took care of his horse, so he returned to the saloon. He had been broke before and would be again. Right now the notion of even tepid nickel beer seemed better than the murky water offered in its stead.

"More whiskey?" asked the skinny barkeep, his eyes darting back and forth between Slocum's face and the six-shooter at his left hip in a cross-draw holster.

"Beer," Slocum said, dropping a dime on the counter.

"You can get two for that," the barkeep said.

"Then set 'em up," Slocum said.

He downed one, and it worked on his thirst. He drank the second more slowly, savoring what there was of its taste. Then he wandered toward the rear of the saloon to watch the poker game. The man with the decent clothes and pile of greenbacks in front of him was drunker than Slocum had first thought. Either that or the time Slocum had been tending his horse had been enough for the man to knock back several shots of liquor and get drunker than a lord.

"I like you boys. Why argue over the pot?" the man said. He shoved the pot into the center of the table. "Divvy it up amongst yourselves. You're all my friends. You *deserve* to share in my bounty."

"What might this bounty be, Colonel Marks?" asked one seedy poker player to the man's right. "You strike it rich up there in the canyon? You gonna make everyone in Albuquerque a rich man with gold or silver?"

"Coal," the drunk man said in a hoarse stage whisper. "Thass-that's all there is in Tijeras Canyon."

"Don't go on with your lyin'," snapped the man to the colonel's left. "We know you found silver up there. Why else can you afford such fancy duds?"

"I am a man of breeding and refinement," the colonel said in drunken haughtiness. "You dare insult me?"

"Where'd you get so much money?" asked the third man at the table, seated across from Marks. Slocum realized the three were working to fleece the drunken colonel. It was robbery, after a fashion, but nothing Slocum was going to get involved in. If Marks hadn't wanted to be fleeced in a poker game, he would never have gotten liquored up and would never have sat down with these owlhoots. It was one thing to help out a man in trouble. It was something else to try to pull a man out of a fire of his own making.

Slocum had learned that lesson well. Such assistance was never appreciated.

He knew better, yet he still got involved.

"You gents mind if I sit in?"

The three glared at him. One sneered, and the other two moved to get to their six-guns more easily. Slocum smiled and pushed in between Marks and the man on his right, the one Slocum pegged as the leader.

"What game are you playing?"

"It's private," said the leader.

"Nonsense, the more the merrier," the colonel declared. "Here, sir, share in my bounty also. You take this." Colonel Marks pushed a pile of greenbacks in Slocum's direction. As Slocum reached for the money, the man across the table half stood and grabbed. Slocum was quicker. His hand shot out like a striking snake and caught the man's brawny wrist.

"He said this was mine, not yours," Slocum said with a smile. The sight was enough to form icicles in the middle of a smithy's forge. The man relented, but with an expression that told Slocum he might have to shoot his way out of this. He was glad he had taken the keeper off the hammer of his Colt.

"What game are we playing?" Slocum looked around the table at each of the men in turn.

"Five-card stud," said the leader, refusing to back down.

"Splendid game," the colonel announced. "I think. I have only this evening learned it, you see. Have I introduced myself, sir? I am sorry. Colonel Thornton Marks, at your service, sir."

"John Slocum." Slocum saw he would have to wait for the Rio Grande to overflow its banks before any of the three others introduced themselves. That was fine with him.

"What brings you to this fine metropolis?" asked Marks, slurring his words slightly.

"Figure to make a few dollars, then move on," Slocum said. "Which is mighty fine advice for you right now, Colonel."

"What? Leave my other friends?"

"They have names?"

"Why, uh, no. I am *so* impolite. I failed to introduce myself around the table. Gents, how do you do? I am Colonel Marks, and I have just this afternoon learned I am the luckiest man alive. My wildest dreams have been answered."

"At the assay office?" the leader asked bluntly.

Marks laughed at this. "Why, no, but the telegrapher did bring me news that a gem more precious than gold is on its way to me."

"Diamond? Ruby?" asked the man across the table.

"Why don't you take a rest, Colonel?" Slocum suggested. "Come on over to the bar. I'll buy you a drink." Slocum smiled wryly. Why not? It was the man's own money he'd be using.

"We're playing," said the unkempt leader. "You butted in where you're not wanted. Now get the hell out of here, mister."

"Slocum," he said, standing. "The name's Slocum." He kicked back the chair and stood, shoulders relaxed and hand at his right hip. But the three saw a steel spring all coiled up and ready to explode. If Slocum drew, he could take out any one of them he wanted—and possibly two. The worn ebony handle on his six-shooter showed years of long, hard use.

Most of all, his attitude deterred them. He was calm, collected, and spoiling for a fight.

"Come on, men," said the leader. "We don't need trouble."

"Yeah, we're gonna tell Billy about this!" The trio left, muttering to themselves.

"Who's Billy?" asked Marks, scratching his head. "Why did they go off like that? I trust I did nothing to make them angry. When I get into one of these moods, I find myself being quite rude at times."

He hiccuped loudly and wobbled in his chair. Slocum slapped him on the back and brought a moment's sobriety to him.

"I don't know who Billy is either, and I think it would be smart if I don't find out." From the silence that had fallen on the crowd in the saloon, he knew better than to stay around much longer. He heaved

Marks to his feet and got the man headed for the rear door.

"Hey, mister," called the scrawny barkeep, "watch your back. Billy Dee's a murderin' son of a bitch. As like to shoot you in the back as look at you."

"Thanks," Slocum said dryly. He found the rear door to be too narrow for a man as drunk as Colonel Thornton Marks. The man bounced from one side to the other, and eventually tumbled through into the alley behind the saloon. The sun had set, casting long cool shadows everywhere. Even the stench of garbage thrown out into the bright sun was beginning to fade a mite.

But Slocum caught another stench right away.

"You, cowboy. Where you goin'? You sneakin' off like the low-down coward you are?"

If Slocum had thought to avoid Billy Dee and his henchmen by leaving through the rear door, he was mistaken. A short man dressed in a flashy brocade vest blocked the exit to the street. He stood with feet planted wide. He cracked the knuckles of his right hand in his left, then dropped his hand to his side, fingers drumming on the soft leather of his holster.

Slocum had seen many a man about ready to throw down on him before. There didn't seem to be any way around bloodshed now. Billy Dee, if that was who he was, was sniffing around for a killing.

"I say, my good man, how are you?" the colonel suddenly said. "Your friends and I were engaged in a poker game. You should come into the saloon and join us. I'll buy."

"You'll buy all right, you old geezer," snapped Billy Dee. "Hand over all your money. You don't have the sense God gave a mule. Let real men spend that money."

"You want it, here, take it," Marks said, stumbling

forward. Slocum grabbed the man's arm and spun him around.

Facing breath strong enough to knock out a boar, Slocum said, "He doesn't care about the money. He wants to kill somebody. Give him the money and he'll still cut you down."

"But—"

Slocum shoved Marks out of the way. The man lost his balance and fell heavily. He was so drunk he couldn't get to his feet easily. That suited Slocum just fine. It kept the man out of the line of fire. If it came to that.

"You must have a reputation around town," Slocum said.

"You've heard of me? Billy Dee, the fastest man in New Mexico Territory."

"No, I just rode into town," Slocum said. The words hung like the miasma over a battlefield. He smelled blood and death.

"You're a fool," Dee said. Behind him came his three henchmen. Slocum noticed them, but kept his attention on Billy Dee. The man was working himself up into a killing rage.

"How many you gunned down?" Slocum asked. "Two? Three?"

"I kilt nine! And you're gonna make number ten."

Billy Dee went for his six-gun. Two shots rang out. A smile came to Dee's face. Then he crumpled to the ground. His six-shooter had discharged in his holster, never clearing leather when Slocum's slug had ripped out his foul heart.

"He was the fastest man I ever seen!" cried a scruffy henchman, staring at the corpse of his boss.

"He wasn't fast enough, not by half," Slocum said, wondering if he would have to kill the other three. They turned and fled, and he cursed as he holstered his six-gun.

If he had killed them where they stood it would have been better. Now they were free to cause mischief. It was time to get out of town before Billy Dee's friends rounded up others in his gang for a little bit of revenge.

2

"I never saw a man react to danger as fast as you just did," Colonel Marks said. His eyes were wide and bloodshot, but he sounded sober. Almost getting a bullet in the gut did that to most men.

"I pulled your fat out of the fire. Now it's time for both of us to leave Albuquerque. Fast," said Slocum. "I don't know how many men Billy Dee had following him around like he was a mama duck and they were his ducklings, but I know of three for sure."

"The ones in the poker game." Marks turned paler now, realizing what a fool he had been. "I have chosen my friends and companions poorly, it would seem."

"So it seems," Slocum said sourly. He stepped out of the alley and looked up and down Railroad Avenue. At the far end of the street stood two powerful steam engines that could move passengers and freight out of town. From the looks of them, though, nothing would be moving for several hours. Slocum had considered taking a train to put as much distance between him and wildly firing six-shooters as possible. But now, in spite of his horse being worn out from the trip north, he knew the valiant animal would have to keep moving—tonight.

"I am Thornton Marks," the man said, thrusting out his hand. "I want to thank you for your services. I am unused to men volunteering for such brutal work."

"Didn't volunteer," Slocum said. He started toward the stables and Marks tagged along. Slocum's quick glances left, right, and behind insured no one was going to ambush him. He wanted the comforting feel of his Winchester in his hands if he got into a real fight. The rifle was a better tool for taking out snipers than his Colt.

"I was a colonel in the British Army. The Raj, you know."

"I don't."

"India." The way Marks said it, the word came out "*In*-jah."

Slocum didn't bother responding. He wanted to get out of town before the lead started flying in his direction. Billy Dee had thought himself a quick hand. He had been wrong. Slocum reckoned the man's nine kills, if he had in fact taken down that many, included murders from ambush, backshooting, and maybe even cutting down unarmed men.

His gang wouldn't be much different.

"Sir," called Marks, his long stride matching Slocum's.

"What?"

"You are not an easy man to thank, are you?"

"I was staying alive. Glad you're still kicking too," said Slocum. He touched his shirt pocket and the wad of greenbacks Marks had given him back in the saloon. Slocum considered returning the money, then decided he had earned it. He peeled off a dollar and stuck it on a nail beside the stall. Grabbing his gear, Slocum began cinching down the saddle on the balky horse.

"Mr. Slocum," Marks said. "That is your name, I seem to remember." He rubbed his head. "I do not usually partake of such potent potables, but tonight I wanted to celebrate.''

"You're not from around here, are you?''

"Why do you say that? Because I am British?''

"Because you didn't know this Billy Dee. He was cock of the walk and obviously the others in the saloon knew it. You didn't.''

"Well, no, I spend most of my time a few dozen miles on the other side of the Sandia Mountains, up in the Tijeras Canyon. That means scissors in Spanish, I believe.''

"I know,'' Slocum said. He led his horse out and started to mount.

"Wait, Mr. Slocum. I need some help. I came to Albuquerque to collect debts owed me. I was very successful in two cases. The third, however, is the largest amount owed me.''

"I'm not a bill collector. See the sheriff. He might consider it akin to serving process.''

"I don't trust him. Or the town marshal. I trust you.''

Slocum fixed the man with a steely gaze. "You're a damn fool. You don't know me from Adam. I'm some drifter who blew into town and wants nothing more than to catch a whirlwind and ride out on it.''

"I read a man's character much better sober than I do drunk,'' Marks admitted. "I did not achieve command in Her Majesty's Fusiliers being careless in such estimates.''

"Hope you didn't spend much time drunk,'' said Slocum. "I'd recommend you get on out of town too.''

He rode from the stable into a ring of leveled six-guns. Slocum considered his options and none of them appeared good. He could never take on so many gunmen, even if he had his six-shooter cocked and ready for action. It hung like an anvil at his left side, a tribute to his foolish urgency to leave town—and not to his caution or good sense.

"This the one, Zeke?" asked a burly unwashed brute in the center of the ring. He stabbed a sawed-off Meteor shotgun in Slocum's direction.

"He shore is. He cut down poor Billy when he wasn't lookin'!"

Slocum knew better than to argue with these men. They had already come to the conclusion that Billy Dee could never die—and when he did, the only possible reason was treachery.

"Good sirs, allow me," said Colonel Marks suddenly. The tall, stately man stepped forward, gripped his left lapel with his left hand, and struck a pose as if he were lecturing a gathering of potential voters. "You do not seek this one. He is, uh, in my employ. You want another man for the death of Mr. Dee."

"What're you goin' on about? I *seen* him gun down Billy!" shouted Zeke. He pointed straight at Slocum.

"No, it was *you*," Colonel Marks said. "Check his weapon. I am sure he is the one who gunned down Mr. Dee. Why would Mr. Slocum do so? He is only recently come to town."

"I thought you said he worked for you."

"He does," Marks went on quickly. "I hired him to look after my financial interests."

"We don't know nothin' about that," said the man with the shotgun. He stared at Zeke, at Marks, and finally at Slocum. He stared at Slocum, fingers drumming on the double triggers, and shouted over his shoulder, "Check Zeke's six-gun."

"Wait, no!" Zeke backed away, his hand going to his gun. "They're tryin' to split us up. I seen him kill Billy. So'd Slim and Mike."

"How about it, Slim? Mike?" asked Slocum, singling out the men in the crowd. "Did you see anything at all?'' He gave them their chance to back off and let the full wrath of Dee's gang fall on Zeke.

"Didn't see anything," said Slim.

"We was still in the saloon," said Mike.

"You lyin' swine!" Zeke went for his gun—and died in a flash of discharging shotguns and rifles.

"An unfortunate occurrence," said Marks, shaking his head. Slocum had to give it to the man. The sight of so much blood did not faze him. Slocum was coming around to believe Thornton Marks actually had been in the British Army and had seen action. Colonel Marks had hardly recoiled at the report from the weapons discharging all at once.

"Get him out of here 'fore the marshal takes it into his head to make trouble," said the man with the still-smoking shotgun. He jerked his head and got the crowd moving.

Slocum dismounted and went to Marks. "Thanks. That was quick thinking. Don't know how much you solved, but it worked—for now."

"I once faced down an entire mob of furious Sikhs, intent on slitting every British throat." Marks touched his neck, and Slocum saw a thin pink line. "Didn't quite succeed with *all* British throats."

"You'd better get on out of town. That Slim and Mike might not say a word, but there's going to be a whale of a lot of trouble as men in the gang try to take it over. Right now the big one's got the upper hand. But he has to sleep sometime."

"You figure this was why he so eagerly assassinated his friend Zeke?"

"Makes sense," said Slocum. The man with the shotgun had eliminated one of Billy Dee's men and increased his own power by doing so. If he ever needed more glue to hold together the gang he had inherited so precipitously, he would come hunting for Slocum and Marks.

"I was not merely, how do you say, beating my gums when I promoted you to my assistant. I need help finding the third man who owes me money—a considerable amount, I should add."

"I don't collect bills."

"I'll make it worth your while. A hundred dollars for a day's work."

Slocum hesitated. The trouble in Albuquerque had passed for the moment. And a hundred dollars, even in scrip, would see him a long way toward Montana. Slocum smiled slightly. Until this moment, he had not realized he had a destination in mind. Reaching Montana with money in his pocket would be a great help, especially since he would be arriving at the edge of winter.

"You are considering my offer. I see it in your face." Marks thrust out his hand. "Shake on it!"

"Who owes you money, how much, and why?" Slocum demanded. He had ridden into a trap because he had failed to be cautious. Before agreeing to ride with Marks, he wanted to know more about the chore.

"The manager of the railroad station," Marks said. "He owes me a thousand dollars for coal I shipped him for use in his steam engines."

"He personally owes you or the railroad he works for?"

"What is the difference? He bought the coal. He pays the bill."

"Fair enough," Slocum said. "You reckon he is in his office this time of night?"

"We can only go to see. The sooner we collect, the sooner I can return to my home."

"I can understand feeling cheerful over that," Slocum said.

"Ah, Mr. Slocum, it is more than homesickness that drives me back to Last Gasp."

"Last Gasp?"

"My town up in the canyon. Coal mines and—"

"Silver too?" Slocum cut in, remembering what the men in the poker game had said.

Thornton Marks heaved a sigh. "Alas, I am not close-lipped enough about my business. Yes, yes, there are two working silver mines pulling out a tiny amount every month. I have other extensive holdings in that otherwise barren stretch. But most important, I need to return to be sure I am there when my, shall we say, *package* arrives."

"What's that?" asked Slocum.

"A very special shipment from back East. Most of my goods come through Santa Fe, or rather the railhead at Lamy."

"This is why you don't come to Albuquerque too often?" asked Slocum.

"Exactly. My business dealings are back East, not in the West."

With Slocum leading his horse, they walked to the railroad office, and Slocum tethered his horse out front. He reached over and made sure his six-shooter slid easily in his holster. He wasn't looking for trouble, but then he hadn't been looking for trouble when he rode into town. His long strides took him up the steps. He bent over and peered into the ticket office. A dim light burned on the table where a young man slept, his head laid across folded arms.

"We're looking for the station manager," Slocum said loudly. The boy shot upright and almost fell from the chair.

"Train's not leavin' till eight A.M.," he said, rubbing his eyes. "We got track problems out west."

"We're looking for..." Slocum turned to Colonel Marks.

"Mr. Thomasen," Marks supplied. "He owes me money."

Slocum frowned. There was no reason to burden the boy with such information, or give Thomasen warning people were coming after him to collect a debt.

"I... I can fetch him for you," the youth said. He ran his hands through longish yellow hair and licked his lips. "This time of night, he wouldn't want to be disturbed, but I can let him know. He ought to be back before the train pulls out."

"Where can we find him?" asked Slocum in a voice that brooked no argument.

"He's got a cot over across the yards. Sleeps there sometimes, but I wouldn't—"

"Thanks, we'll find it ourselves," Slocum said. He grabbed Marks by the arm and steered the former British officer away from the ticket office in the depot.

"What's wrong, Mr. Slocum? We—"

"Shut up. You go shooting off your mouth like that and we might never find Thomasen."

"He is an agent of this railroad. Of course we will find him."

Slocum glanced over his shoulder and saw the ticket agent had summoned a hard-looking man, possibly a railroad detective. Marks seemed to be a lightning rod for trouble. As they hurried across the tracks around the long trains, Slocum amended that. Everything Marks said brought the wrath of the heavens down on them. It wasn't that he was an iron pole sticking up into the sky. But he inadvertently thrust one up, thinking he was doing well.

"There's the shack," Slocum said. A tiny kerosene lamp lit one window. Rubbing dirt from the pane, Slocum peered in and saw why the ticket agent had been reluctant to fetch his boss. Thomasen lay naked on the cot with an unclothed young woman, probably a whore from some nearby bagnio.

As Slocum turned, he caught sight of dark forms moving in the shadows through the rail yard. He pushed Marks one direction and dove the other as a heavy length of pipe crashed into the shack. Splinters flew as the lead pipe buried itself in the rotted wood.

Slocum hit the ground, rolled, and came to his knees, fists flying. He felt his left hand collide with a belt buckle. He winced and swung his right fist a few inches higher. He was rewarded with a loud *oof!* and felt his attacker staggering away. Slocum swarmed up, grabbed an ax handle dropped on the ground, and used it to put the man out. Swinging around, Slocum smashed the oak shaft into another man's midriff. He buckled, dropping a length of chain.

Slocum gauged distances the best he could in the dark, then kicked and caught the man in the face. Neither of his attackers was likely to bother him further. But he saw two others had grabbed Marks. Slocum raced to the man's assistance, only to find Marks was capable of defending himself. He had punched out one man, and was squaring off against the second, when Slocum arrived. A short swing of the ax handle ended the fight.

"There was no need to attack from the rear, Mr. Slocum," Colonel Marks said, panting harshly. Slocum wondered how old Marks was. At first blush, the man was middle-aged, yet his boasts of duty in India belied that. Now that he had put himself out, Slocum saw the years etched on the man's face. He might be fifty or even older.

"We don't need to dally with them. We're after Thomasen, remember?"

"I do, sir. Allow me to catch my breath."

Slocum did no such thing. He went to the shack and

kicked open the door. It flew inward, coming off its hinges as nails tore out of the thin wood. On the sagging cot, Thomasen was sitting up. When he saw Slocum in the doorway, oak stave in hand, he let out a yelp and shoved the naked woman onto the floor in his haste to grab a six-gun on the table next to the lamp.

Slocum lifted the ax handle and brought it down, smashing the table and sending the gun flying.

"Get out of here," Slocum said to the woman.

"My clothes," she said. "Let me get dressed."

"Take them with you. I have business with Mr. Thomasen."

Slocum kicked some of the woman's clothing in her direction as she knelt and grabbed at her scattered raiment. He stood over the cot, glaring at the stationmaster. Only when the woman had left did Slocum speak.

"You owe Colonel Marks some money. It's time to pay up."

Thomasen swallowed hard. His eyes darted about, hunting for any way out. Slocum made sure all avenues of exit were blocked, swinging his ax handle and then thwacking it hard into his callused palm.

"Forty tons of coal, sir," said Marks from the doorway. "You were to pay within a month. It has been ninety days and still I await your payment."

"I ain't got the money. I . . . the company wouldn't send it from the home office."

"Then I'll have to decide how much blood and pain equals what you owe the colonel," Slocum said. "One thousand dollars worth of suffering puts you in the class where an Apache brave's stomach might turn at what I'll do to you."

"Wait, wait, you don't understand. I don't have it."

"Why not?" asked Marks almost gently.

"I got it from Kansas City but I—but I lost it in a card game!"

"You spent it on loose women," suggested Marks. "You lost it in a game of chance. You frittered it away in a dozen different ways rather than pay me. A shame. I rather liked you, Mr. Thomasen."

Slocum heard the tone Colonel Marks used. It was his cue to get tough. He lifted the ax handle and brought it crashing down, missing Thomasen's head by inches and breaking the cot. The station manager fell heavily to the floor.

"Wait, don't, I can get the money! I can!"

"We need it right now," Slocum said. "Can you get it right now?"

"Yes, yes," begged Thomasen. "I need to get it from the office safe."

"Lead the way," Slocum said. He kicked Thomasen's shoes from his grasp. "You can get your clothes later. After the colonel gets his money."

"But I have nothing on!"

"That's perfectly obvious," Marks said with a chuckle. Then he sobered. "That makes no difference to us. On your way, Thomasen. The sooner you pay me, the sooner you can get back to your dalliances."

Picking his way across the rail yard, cinders cutting his bare feet, the naked man reached the depot. The young man stared at his boss, eyes wide, as he made his way to the safe and worked the combination. It took Thomasen three tries before he got it right. Inside stood tall stacks of greenbacks. Slocum licked his lips. Tempting.

"How much does he owe you, Colonel?"

"Eight hundred dollars for the coal," Marks said, "and another two hundred for shipping. I had two wagons break down on the way here."

"That's robbery!" yelled the station manager.

"Robbery would be taking all that money," Slocum said. "All Colonel Marks wants is his due."

"I helped you out of a serious supply problem," Marks said. "You did not haggle over the price when we reached our agreement. You will not whimper now as you pay me one thousand dollars."

Reluctantly, the naked Thomasen counted out the money. Marks made him count it a second time, then counted it himself. The station manager glared at his ticket agent. The youth hid a smile and averted his eyes.

"Precisely done," Marks congratulated. He scribbled out a note, signed it with a flourish, and handed it to the naked man. "Your receipt, sir. Everything is properly done. Now it is time to go home and see if my special package has arrived. Mr. Slocum?"

Slocum kicked the door to the safe shut and spun the dial, then dropped the oak stave to the floor. He left with Marks, feeling the hot glare on his back.

It made him feel good knowing justice, however small, had been served this night.

3

"Here you are, Mr. Slocum," said Colonel Marks, counting out one hundred dollars in tens from the bankroll he had taken from Thomasen. "You have done well and aided my cause admirably. Thank you."

Slocum considered the trouble Marks had caused along the way. They might have avoided the railroad detectives and the ensuing fight entirely if the man had kept his mouth shut. Slocum didn't blame the young man in the ticket agent's cage for calling in the four detectives. Marks had made it impossible for him to do otherwise.

Slocum remembered what he had thought about lightning rods and Colonel Thornton Marks. It struck him as all the more appropriate. What was the station manager likely to do now? What were the four railroad detectives likely to do? And the rattlers nest of gunmen who had once pledged allegiance to Billy Dee might prove even nastier.

"Time to ride on," Slocum said. His horse nickered and gave a little shudder of disbelief. Slocum patted the horse's neck. "I know it's hard, but it's the safest thing right now."

"I say, are you talking to me or your mount? Ah, yes, I see. Your horse. I quite agree, however, that remaining in this fair town is a mistake." Marks cleared his throat and looked around. Albuquerque was slowly closing up for the night. It had to be after midnight.

"Spit it out," Slocum said.

"Would you accompany me as far as Last Gasp? I know this is an imposition, Mr. Slocum, but it is hardly out of your way if you travel north. We need only go a few miles east, then turn into the canyon. That will take you directly to Santa Fe and onward."

Slocum's hands pressed into the bills in his shirt pocket. He had almost two hundred dollars, all from Colonel Marks.

"If it doesn't take me too far out of my way," he heard himself saying. Then he shook his head at such stupidity. He ought to put as much distance between him and the trouble-prone colonel as possible.

"It will not, and I assure you of a splendid reception in my town. In all the towns along the road!"

"Let's ride," Slocum said.

Marks rode his gray sitting ramrod straight, precise and formal as a British officer ought to be. Slocum rode to one side, watching the road. They went south through the Chinese section. He saw the women already slaving away in the laundries, and caught a hint of the opium smoke drifting from opium dens. He doubted any but the proprietors in them were from the Flowery Kingdom. Celestials sometimes used the drug, but more often sold it to others not of their race.

He shrugged it off. The sale of the potent narcotic probably kept dozens of Chinese alive in the jerkwater town.

The road began curving to the southeast, and finally it took them due east into the foothills. The path through the canyon grew more rugged until they reached the end of the Sandia Mountains. The road heading north on the side of the mountains opposite Albuquerque proved more level and rock-free than any Slocum had encountered in a month of Sundays.

"Got to maintain the road for my coal shipments," Marks said. He pointed up the slopes of the mountains rising steeply on either side. In the dim early morning light, Slocum saw the tailings falling down the mountainsides like giant rock fingers pointing at him. He shivered and didn't know why.

"Generally, the coal is sold at Lamy. I allowed myself to be gulled by that Thomasen into believing I might find a new market." Marks snorted imperiously. "Never again will I deal with his like. Cash on the barrelhead, as they say."

"A good idea," Slocum said. He rubbed the back of his neck and shivered again. The hairs had risen. Throughout the war he had survived because his sixth sense warned him of danger. He wasn't sure that was happening now, but he wasn't comfortable. That alone was enough to make him rein back and slowly scan the terrain ahead and to the sides.

"Is there a problem, Mr. Slocum? I am anxious to get to Last Gasp. My package . . ."

". . . might have arrived," Slocum finished for him. "You mentioned that. More than once."

"I am so eager. Please excuse an old man's enthusiasm. I have gone throughout my life alone. My parents died when I was young. Sandhurst became my family until I entered the Queen's service. Then the army provided all the nurturing I required. I am entering the twilight years and feel most exquisitely this lack of more intimate family."

"No brothers or sisters?"

"None, sir."

Slocum paused a moment, his thoughts going to Robert. Would he have been better off not having a brother so brutally slaughtered? The answer came quickly enough. The times he had spent with his brother growing up, hunting, farming, swimming in the pond on the corner of their land, all of it outweighed the pain of loss.

"Someone's trailing us," Slocum said suddenly. He saw nothing, but some faint sound had alerted him. Or was it the lack of any sound? No birds gave voice to their mournful songs, no rabbits scurried about, no deer poked a nose out of the underbrush.

"Road agents?"

"Possibly. More likely, someone from Albuquerque we irritated a mite too much."

"I find that list to be an extensive one," Marks said with some humor. "Should we go to ground, perhaps find refuge in one of the mines? These are all petered out. My coal mining operations have moved farther north, toward Last Gasp."

"If we hole up, that might be the last thing we do," Slocum decided. He didn't have much ammunition with him, certainly not enough for a major fight. "It's better to get on into your town where we might get help."

"I don't have much of a marshal. And the sheriff never comes this far up into the canyon from Albuquerque. What law we see is mostly from Santa Fe."

"Don't much care where they hail from," Slocum said, urging his exhausted horse to a quicker gait. "If they can shoot straight, that's good enough for me."

"Is our situation so serious?" Colonel Marks turned in the saddle and studied the backtrail. "I see nothing to indicate brigands pursue us."

"Neither do I," Slocum admitted. "Might be spooked for no reason, but I don't think so."

"We are still ten miles or more from Last Gasp. I had hoped to rest my horse and perhaps water her."

Slocum argued with himself about this. He saw nothing, but the feeling of pursuit grew more intense. Resting their horses would let them reach Last Gasp without any chance of killing the mounts under them. If he pressed on now, both of them might be afoot—and for no good reason other than a vague feeling.

"There a watering hole around here?" Slocum asked.

"Several stock tanks nearby," said Marks. "A few minutes' leisure cannot possibly be amiss after our all-night ride."

"Go on," Slocum said, reaching for his rifle. "Show the way."

Marks rode off the road and down a dirt path hardly more than a game trail. It wound through the salt cedar and cottonwoods before suddenly opening on a shallow depression. Slocum's quick glance showed nothing but cattle hooves had cut into the dirt here.

"I have a few small herds of beeves," Marks explained.

"You sound as if you own the entire canyon."

"Perhaps not all," Marks admitted, "but much of it is mine, I am pleased to say."

Cattle, coal and silver mines, an entire damned town. Thornton Marks was far more than he seemed. Slocum swung from the saddle, taking his rifle with him. He let his worn-down horse drink, wondering how soon he ought to pull the gelding back.

A few feet away, Marks let his gray noisily slurp up water while he knelt and cupped his hands, bringing the muddy water to his lips.

Slocum was almost blinded by the flash from the rifle. He stared directly into the thicket behind Marks, but saw no hint of the sniper lying in wait there. The foot-long tongue of orange flame left blue and yellow dots dancing in Slocum's vision, but this didn't stop him from lifting his own rifle and firing.

He had no clear target. Firing simply to drive back the sniper wasn't much of a plan, but he hoped it would be enough to give him and Marks time to find cover.

"This way," Slocum hissed to the colonel. "We have to get under cover."

The man continued to kneel, not moving.

"What's wrong? Dammit, come on!" Slocum fired twice more in the direction of the first shot as he raced to Marks's side. The man toppled to the ground, clutching himself. A large red spot spread slowly on Marks's coat.

"I do believe I am hit, Mr. Slocum," came the colonel's weak voice. "This is the first time I have been wounded, and it feels so . . . different."

Slocum flopped onto his belly when new rounds ripped through the air just above his head. Marks's horse let out a neigh and a gasp, then fell into the watering hole, dead.

"I cannot move, sir," Marks said.

"Hang on," Slocum said. He got his arm around Marks and heaved, throwing the man bodily over the carcass of the dead horse. Using its bulk as a shield would work for a few minutes—until their attacker flanked them or even got to the far side of the pond and shot at them from there.

When two slugs sang past Slocum's head, he realized more than one bushwhacker was attacking them.

"We're in trouble," he told Marks. "We're up against at least two gunmen. I get the feeling there's at least one more out there, laying low until he can get us in his sights."

"I feel cold, Mr. Slocum. My hands are trembling also." Marks held out his shaking hands, then let them drop. "I need to get to Last Gasp. My package must have arrived by now. It can't be kept waiting. I must not let it sit untended."

"First things first," Slocum said. He rested his rifle on the side of Marks's dead horse. His own had run off. He heard the gelding neighing in protest not far away. Waiting, waiting, waiting, Slocum bided his time until he got a good shot. When he saw a hand balancing a rifle stock in it, he fired.

He smiled wryly at the loud yelp of pain. He had winged the man, not killed him. But it would keep the attackers at bay for a spell. What worried Slocum most was how exposed he and the colonel were to the rear. Anyone in the thicket on the far side of the pond had an easy shot at their backs.

"We can't stay," Slocum told Marks. He reached down and felt the pulse in the man's throat. Slocum worried the man might have died on him. A faint, thready pulse told him the old soldier still lived. And the strong hand gripping his wrist convinced Slocum there was more than a trace of fight left in Thornton Marks.

"Then let's go," Marks said. "It is what we both desire most, Mr. Slocum." The voice was strong, but the hand gripping his wrist weakened rapidly.

"I've got to flush them out." Slocum hesitated. "You have any idea who they might be?"

"Does it matter?" Marks looked up with surprisingly clear eyes. "They want to kill us. Friend or foe, Billy Dee's gang or thugs sent by Thomasen, does it really matter one whit?"

"No," Slocum said, launching himself. He ran bent over, dodging the slugs tearing past him. He almost reached the cover provided by a blackberry bush when a bullet caught him high on the thigh, sending him tumbling. He hit the ground hard, lost his rifle, and rolled, trying to regain it. A fusillade drove him away from his Winchester and to the insubstantial shelter offered by the thorny plant.

He winced when a second piece of burning lead found a target. A chunk of his upper left forearm was shot off, sending a shower of blood down his arm. It looked worse than it felt, but Slocum knew he had to get it bandaged soon or he might weaken. He flexed the muscle and winced at the pang stabbing into his shoulder. It distracted him, but knowing he would die if he gave in to the pain kept him directed at the pair of backshooters hidden not twenty yards away.

This was no time to betray frailty. Slocum drew his Colt Navy and peered past the berry bush in time to see a flash of red in the morning sun. A bandanna carelessly worn—or was it? A slow smile came to Slocum's lips. They thought to gull him into wasting his ammo on a bandanna waved at the end of a stick.

Backtracking along what must be the stick where the cloth was knotted, Slocum spotted the man behind the simple ruse. Slocum took a deep, settling breath. He fired three quick shots and knew at a gut level he had made a clean kill. The fluttering red bandanna vanished from sight.

"He got 'im!" came the whining protest from somewhere to the left of the felled man with the bandanna. "You said we'd—"

"Shut up!" came the harsh command from a few yards on the other side of the thicket. Slocum listened carefully, trying to pick out any other ambushers. There had been three. Now only two remained. And he had three rounds ready for them.

Slocum squeezed off another round in the direction of the owlhoot doing the most complaining. He doubted the slug came close, but the man was ready to turn and hightail it now that he thought Slocum had his range.

"Rush 'im," came the cold command. "He's out of ammo."

"You do it," argued the other man. "How do you

know he's not got more rounds, just waitin' to drill us?''

"I've been counting."

This decided Slocum. The man had made a mistake or wanted his partner to end up dead, possibly leaving an easier target for his own deadly fire. His ignorance or his duplicity meant nothing. Slocum decided to launch a frontal assault. It was foolhardy, but he had no chance to save Colonel Marks any other way. He could have sneaked off into the stand of trees and abandoned the wounded man, but that wasn't Slocum's way.

If he left behind a wounded man to be killed by road agents, Slocum would never have slept peacefully again.

"Aieeee!" he shouted like a battle-crazy Apache, running forward as hard and fast as he could. He fired again, knowing he had only one round remaining in his Colt Navy.

"Get him, shoot him, do it now!" came the frantic cry.

Both men rose from hiding, presenting Slocum with a dilemma. Which was the boss and which the follower? Kill the leader and the other would crumple like a house of cards. He got off a shot at the man on his left and knew instantly he had fired at the wrong one.

"I'll get him!"

Slocum started to hit the ground and roll to present as small a target as he could. To his surprise two sharp, high-pitched reports sounded, driving the leader back to cover.

Slocum saw Colonel Marks holding a small derringer, both barrels smoking. He had not known the man carried the vest-pocket weapon.

From the sound of the crashing and thrashing going on, those shots had convinced both men to get the hell out. Slocum dropped to his knees and took a deep, slow breath to calm his racing heart. He had been within seconds of death. A single shot—a moment of bravery on the part of his attackers—and he would have died.

Horses' hooves pounding off into the distance told him the danger had passed. He stood and searched through the undergrowth. He found the dropped bandanna, but not the man he was sure he had killed. He frowned. The two might have taken their fallen comrade. If so, he might never know who had bushwhacked them.

Slocum knew he could find enough evidence to identify his attackers, but it would take considerable work. He had to get Thornton Marks to a doctor before the man died. For all that, Slocum's own wounds bled freely, making him giddy.

Staggering back on a leg now almost too weak to support him, Slocum realized he had been running on nothing but piss and vinegar. He fell heavily beside Marks.

"Thanks. You saved my neck out there."

The derringer had slipped from nerveless fingers. Marks turned his eyes toward Slocum, shocking him. Marks had been alert before. Now his eyes were unfocused.

"I'll get you to Last Gasp and your mysterious parcel."

"I know, Mr. Slocum. You are the one to do it. If anyone can, you will."

Somehow Slocum got Marks belly-down over the saddle on the gelding. Try as he might, he could not mount behind Marks. Slocum's wounded leg would not let him. Hobbling along, leaning heavily on his complaining horse, Slocum headed up the canyon in the direction of Last Gasp.

4

Sunset. Slocum was sure it was sunset. Or was he turned around and it was actually morning? He shook his head and rubbed his eyes to clear them. Somehow, they refused to focus. He clung tenaciously to the saddlehorn, aware of the intermittent groans of Thornton Marks. The old colonel was tougher than he looked, Slocum thought.

Then his mind wandered. He limped heavily, hardly able to stand. And his left arm stung as if a million ants had decided he was a fitting supper. Sweat poured down his face and burned his eyes, but he kept moving. He had to. Last Gasp lay ahead.

"Last Gasp," Slocum grunted, amused and appalled at the unintended meaning it might hold. It was Marks's town. It might also be his last resting place.

One foot in front of the other. Step, drag his right leg. Step, drag.

"My pretty package. I must be there," Marks called out in a voice stronger than Slocum would have thought possible. Slocum had drained his canteen, having forgotten to fill it before leaving the watering hole. He hadn't been thinking clearly then, and certainly was not now. He made bad decisions, and he burned up with fever. But he had to keep moving.

He had to get to Last Gasp because Marks expected a package from back East.

"What happened to you?"

The voice echoed in the back of Slocum's head.

"You know. You were there. Bushwhacking sons of bitches," Slocum grated out. "Save your breath, Colonel. We're not far from your town. I feel it."

"What you sayin', mister?"

"Need to get to Last Gasp. It's only another mile or two up the canyon. Good road. To the coal mines, you said?"

"I ain't said nothin' to you, mister. Hey, Doc!" went up the shout. "We got a pair of 'em for your butcher shop. One looks to be the colonel!"

Slocum stopped and clung weakly to his horse. The animal shifted its weight, and he fell heavily. Lying in the dirt, he found he had no more strength to get up. He would die out on the road, in the middle of nowhere. He had failed Colonel Marks.

Slocum closed his eyes and let himself float upward. Then he passed out when something hard and heavy crashed into his head.

"You back to the land of the living?" said a gruff voice.

"I am," Slocum said, blinking to get his eyes clear and focused. Everything was blurry, but he smelled the sharp odor of carbolic acid. Running his hand back and forth told him he lay on cotton sheets.

"Don't go opening that wound on your arm again. I don't have another set of sheets that aren't all blood-stained. Damned shame the way the only ones who make it to my office are always bleeding like stuck pigs."

"Yeah, right, Doc. They can't wait for you to finish them off."

The second voice was lighter in tone, bantering. Slocum pushed up to his elbows, the pain in his left biceps finally bringing everything into focus for him. He lay on a cot in a doctor's office. In a more comfortable bed across the room lay a snoring Thornton Marks.

"He made it?"

"No thanks to Doc Newton," said the pleasant, sandy-haired middle-aged man sitting with his feet propped up on the corner of the doctor's desk. He dropped his feet and came to sit on the cot beside Slocum. "You and the colonel been through Hell from the look of it. You said you'd been bushwhacked? Who did it?"

Slocum shook his head and immediately regretted it. He touched a lump the size of a goose egg on the side of his head. He didn't remember getting it.

"The boys were a bit too eager getting you into my surgery," Doc Newton said. "They whumped your head good against the door bringing you in. Sorry about that."

"Might have been a boon to you, since the doc used the last of his anesthetic on the colonel."

"How is he?"

"You got him back alive." The man shook his head. "More 'n that, I can't tell. And the doctor refuses to make any guarantees."

Slocum saw the grim expression on Doc Newton's face and knew the outlook wasn't good for Marks. He tried to swing his legs around and get his feet under him, but the sandy-haired man pushed him back gently.

"Son, I'm the town's banker, and I know when an account is approaching overdrawn. You don't want to get out of bed, not for a while."

"Ben, that you, Ben?" called Thornton Marks from

the other side of the room. The banker glared at Slocum to keep him in his place, then went to Marks.

"I'm here, Colonel."

"Doc Newton?"

"I'm here also. You rest."

"Get the marshal, if you can sober him up."

"Marshal Dawkins is over at the jailhouse. He actually arrested himself a cattle rustler," said Ben.

"Rustler?"

"The Young lad. Caught him red-handed with one of your beeves."

"The Youngs are starving to death. The boy was only taking the cow to feed his family," said Marks. "Dawkins is a fool, but I need him here. Do it, Ben. Now. For me." Colonel Marks's voice weakened. The banker motioned to a towheaded boy standing in the doorway of the surgery. The boy raced off, returning with a potbellied man wearing a battered star hammered crudely out of a silver Mexican peso.

"Heard tell you was waylaid, Colonel," said the marshal. "That the varmint over there?"

"Shut up, Dawkins," Marks said with rancor. "That man saved my life. More 'n once, I might add. I want you, Ben, and the doctor to listen up real close."

Slocum strained to hear what Marks said, but the man's voice weakened to the point that he heard only strained breathing. Then Colonel Thornton Marks jerked, reached out, and caught at Dr. Newton's arm before slumping back.

The doctor pulled up the sheet and dropped it over the dead man's face.

"Looks like you brung him back for nothin', Mr. Slocum," said the marshal.

"He was tougher than he looked. Reckon he really was a colonel in the Queen's army."

"He was all that and more, much more, Mr. Slocum,"

said the banker. Ben chewed at his lower lip, looking from the marshal to the doctor and back to Slocum. "You impressed him a sight more 'n most folks in Last Gasp. He said you had common sense."

Slocum touched the bloodstained pocket where the money he had gotten from Marks rested. Almost two hundred dollars. It was too much because he had not brought the man home in one piece.

"Damn shame he had to die. I'm not sure they wanted him dead."

"Might have been a kidnap attempt," opined the doctor.

Marshal Dawkins stared at the floor, as if this would absolve him of all blame. "Better get a posse formed and go huntin' for them. You help out, Slocum?"

"Of course," Slocum said. "I'll show you the watering hole and from there we can track them down. How long's it been since morning?"

"Two hours," said the banker. "You got in yesterday afternoon. That makes the trail a day old, and maybe more by the time you get there. But this isn't going to be necessary, Marshal. Is it?"

"Why not?" Slocum sat straighter. He had heard men being railroaded before. This had the same ring to it— and he was the one most likely to have his neck stretched by a length of hemp fastened on a tree limb.

Ben heaved a sigh and said, "You willing to take on the chore of tracking down the cowards who killed the colonel?"

"Yes," Slocum said. He rubbed his leg and winced at the pain darting into his foot. "I owe them personally. And for Marks."

"You know the colonel didn't have any family in these parts." Ben cleared his throat. "Might be he didn't have any family anywhere."

"He said he was alone in the world," Slocum allowed.

"You stand to inherit his poke."

Slocum's eyebrows rose. "The coal and silver mines?"

"They're not worth as much as it sounds. Mostly, they've petered out. The coal mines are the best of the lot, I'd reckon. You can see for yourself."

"The herd of cattle?" asked Slocum.

"He has some," said Ben.

"Then give the cow to the Young boy. It's what the colonel would have wanted."

"No!" protested the marshal. "I caught him fair and square. He stole that walking pile of skin and bones and—"

"I heard the colonel," Slocum said. "Even if I hadn't, the colonel's not around to press charges. And I won't. Give the boy a second cow of his choice."

The marshal left the surgery, grumbling to himself. Both the banker and the doctor broke out laughing when he had left.

"Yes, sir, I think the colonel hit the bull's-eye. You *are* the right one to inherit everything."

"There's one other thing you have to promise to do before getting the colonel's estate," said Dr. Newton. "You have to agree to take care of the package he had coming down from the railhead at Lamy."

"He spoke constantly of it," Slocum said. "I owe him that much. I can do it."

"I'm glad you know what he was talking about," sighed the banker. "I thought he might have been a bit delirious at the end."

"What exactly have I inherited?" Slocum asked.

The banker and doctor looked at each other, then laughed.

"Why, Mr. Slocum, you inherit everything."

"What do you mean?"

"The mines along the canyon walls, the cattle wandering over the land, the land itself, the whole shebang. You now own every last dilapidated building, every splinter of wood, every horse and chicken, the bank and most all the money in its vault, the businesses and all their stock, everything in the town of Last Gasp. You own *us*!"

"You're getting around pretty good, Mr. Slocum," said the banker. Ben Longbaugh pushed a chair in Slocum's direction so he could sit down. Slocum rested the cane fashioned for him by the town's only carpenter against the banker's desk.

"I'm on the mend. I need to heal so I can get on with my job."

"Your job's running the town. We don't have a mayor. Don't need one since you make the decisions."

"Don't much need a lawman either," Slocum said. Twice in the past week he had ridden out with Marshal Dawkins in a vain attempt to find the bushwhackers responsible for killing Colonel Marks. The lawman was even more inept on the trail than he was in town. Circling the watering hole had shown how the ambush had developed, where the men had hidden, and why Slocum had been drawn into the trap. The three attacking him and Marks had not been as smart as they'd been lucky.

Or maybe they knew the terrain.

It didn't matter because Dawkins had nothing to lend to the effort, and Slocum had found only tracks going across a rocky stretch. But he now remembered the face of one of the bushwhackers who'd escaped. Slim, one of the owlhoots from the card game back in Albuquerque. Had he been out to avenge Billy Dee's death? Or had he been working for someone else? Maybe Thomasen?

"Marshal's all we need usually," said Ben. "The sight of a man wearing a badge and a gun is enough to keep the peace. Usually. Dave Dawkins isn't a bad man, just an incompetent one."

"I'll be after the killers soon. You have any more idea who might wish the colonel harm?"

"Just the folks I've mentioned," said the banker. "The colonel could be abrasive when it came to business. He was a hard dealer who sometimes gave people the wrong idea about his intentions."

"I noticed he tended to share his personal business a mite too quick," said Slocum. He was still astounded at the sheer wealth he controlled in Last Gasp. He *owned* the town. And it made him increasingly uneasy. He left most of the day-to-day business in Ben Longbaugh's capable hands since much of the actual commerce lay beyond his own understanding.

"About the opposite of you, I'd say," observed the banker.

"This isn't any fit way to live. I've been thinking about changing things around so that you—"

"Mr. Slocum! Mr. Slocum!" came the loud cry from the bank entrance. "You got a telegram waiting for you at the Western Union. Real important, Mr. Pond said."

"I'll be right there," Slocum said, heaving to his feet. His leg supported him better now. Doc Newton had done a good job patching him up. He stared down at the banker, considering what he intended doing. He was not cut out to be a landowner, certainly not the owner of an entire town. He intended to deed it over to the people actually using the property, and even give the bank and its assets to Longbaugh. But later. The telegrapher had a wire for him, and this puzzled him.

"What should we do about the last of the silver mines?" asked the banker. "I recommend shuttering them."

"How many miners working them?" Slocum had spent too much of his life toiling in mines. He had always hated it when the vein petered out—and so did the job. Working underground was backbreaking, poorly paid work.

"A dozen. Why?"

"Any of the coal mines need workers?"

"I'll check with the foreman over at the Black Beauty mine." Ben Longbaugh stared at Slocum a second, then grinned. "Yes, sir, the colonel picked a winner in you. Most men would say 'throw the rock-breaking bastards out on their ear,' but not you."

Slocum shrugged. It was hardly a favor he was doing for the men, trading one hole in the ground for another. Mining coal might even be worse, with the soot and ever-present danger of fire. Still, better for the men to choose their fate than be tossed about like a leaf on a spring-swollen creek.

He used his cane less and less as he walked, and felt stronger for it. He reached the Western Union office and poked his head inside. "Mr. Pond, I got word of a wire."

"Here it is, Mr. Slocum. I'm not sure what this means. Old Charley at the Santa Fe office always was something of a kidder, but I can't make head nor tail of this."

He thrust the flimsy yellow sheet across the counter. Slocum hobbled over and read it. He frowned a moment, then shrugged.

"The colonel's package from back East will be arriving at the AT&SF depot in Lamy tomorrow noon." Slocum folded the telegram and thrust it into his pocket. "Reckon I'll go pick it up personally since it meant so much to him."

"You be careful now, you hear, Mr. Slocum?"

warned the telegrapher. "Those owlhoots are still out there. They might try to finish what they started with the colonel."

"Thanks, Mr. Pond," Slocum said, amazed at the way the people of Last Gasp cleaved together. The sense of community was something he had not experienced since before the war back in Calhoun County, Georgia.

Slocum made a quick circuit of the town, speaking to the citizens, then got his horse and rode north. In a way, for the first time in years, Slocum felt as if he was leaving home. He shook off the feeling and rode a little faster. He wanted to meet the train when it pulled into the station the next day.

Slocum stretched his stiff leg. Riding had caused him a spot of pain, but nothing as bad as he felt now. He thrust the leg in front of him and massaged it until the pain eased up.

"Mr. Slocum, that's the train steamin' in now!" called the Lamy stationmaster. In the distance rose a plume of white smoke from the smokestack. He saw no reason to stand until the train spat sparks from its drive wheels and screeched to a halt. He wasn't sure who he ought to see about cargo. He started down the platform in the direction of the mail car. Marks would have had anything important sent under lock and key.

"You Colonel Marks?" called the conductor, swinging off the train.

"I've come to pick up his property," Slocum said.

The conductor frowned and started to speak, then clamped his mouth shut as a tall, trim dark-haired woman with the most enchanting emerald eyes he had ever seen pushed past to stand on the platform.

"Wasn't Thornton able to come himself?" the woman asked.

"I'm John Slocum," he said, introducing himself. "Who might you be?"

"Why," she said, smiling brightly, "my name is Helen Frederickson. And I'm the colonel's bride."

Slocum stared, not sure what to say.

5

John Slocum took off his hat and wiped sweat from his face. It was a hot New Mexico day, but not nearly as hot as the spot he found himself in right now.

"Didn't know the colonel had a bride," he said, struggling to find the words. Helen Frederickson smiled brightly. She looked to be in her late twenties and dignified, the sort who would marry a former colonel in the British Army. A woman like her would seem more at home in Boston serving afternoon tea and talking with ladies of high society rather than roughing it out West.

She surely did not fit into the rough-and-tumble life of a town like Last Gasp.

"Oh, I've come here to be married to Thornton. Why was he detained? He promised me in a half-dozen letters he would be here personally to greet me." She smiled almost shyly. "It's not every day a woman gets to meet her betrothed, after all."

"You're a mail-order bride?" Slocum asked.

"Well, that is a rather uncouth way of putting it, but I assume it fits the definition. Thornton and I have never met. We corresponded, having been introduced through a mutual friend. My situation changed radically and I agreed to marry him.''

''Sight unseen?''

''I suppose so, but there is so much to him. I know him to be a loving, caring man from all he has said and done. In a way, he is taking a bigger chance with me than I with him.'' Helen cocked her head to one side, then asked, ''You seem in the dark about all this, Mr. Slocum. What *has* Thornton told you?''

''Not a great deal. Miss Frederickson, please, sit down over here.'' He guided her to the simple bench at the end of the platform. She frowned, but went along.

''This is not some prank, is it? I am not amused!''

''I wish it was a bad joke. I only met the colonel a couple weeks back, so all I know of him is sketchy. But one thing he did make clear. He wanted to be here today to greet you.''

''What's wrong, Mr. Slocum?''

''I don't mean to shock you, but I've found that sugary words don't do much to ease pain.'' Slocum took a deep breath and told her. He watched the ripples of emotion cross her lovely face. At first she seemed to deny her betrothed was dead. Then she seemed to accept it and sink into herself, becoming smaller and somehow more fragile.

Any hint of pleasure vanished.

''He was murdered?''

''You could call it that. We were riding into Last Gasp from Albuquerque when we were drygulched,'' Slocum said. ''I recognized one of the men doing the shooting from Albuquerque, and I reckon I killed another one of them.''

''Were you injured?''

''Not too bad.'' Even as he told the lie, his leg gave him a twinge of pain and his left arm began to itch. He had healed fast, both wounds being clean. What had yet to heal was his outrage at being gunned down the way he had been. Slocum would get his vengeance, and it wasn't entirely for Thornton Marks.

Helen Frederickson turned from him and stared out into the desert. Slocum wondered what ran through her mind. He respected her need for silence and honored it. After a spell, he cleared his throat to get her attention.

"Would you like me to get you a ticket back to . . ." Slocum let his words trail off. He had no idea where Helen had come from. Simply because he thought she was a highfalutin society lady didn't mean it was so. She had bubbled over with enthusiasm and real eagerness to see a man she'd meant to marry after corresponding with him. Slocum knew nothing at all about her— or the kind of a woman who would do a thing like that.

"I don't have the money for a return ticket," she said simply.

"That's no problem," Slocum said, still not used to his newfound riches. He could buy her a hundred tickets and not touch the wealth left to him by Colonel Marks.

"I do not accept charity." She sat with firm chin high and her red lips thinned to a line. "All my life there has been nothing but one misfortune after another. Never have I given in to it, and I shall not now."

"There's nothing for you here in Lamy," Slocum said. "Santa Fe isn't much better. I can arrange for a place for you to stay in Last Gasp, if you want."

"I want to see Thornton's grave, if this is possible." She shuddered.

"Why shouldn't it?" Slocum asked.

"I know nothing of the circumstances of his death. Maybe buzzards ate him or something." Her eyes turned skyward as she spotted two circling carrion-eaters hunting for dinner.

"He died in the doctor's office. Doc Newton did all

he could, but there comes a time when a man rides past any doctor's skill.''

"I did not mean anything untoward happened. I . . . this is all too sudden for me."

"Me too," said Slocum. "I came here thinking I was fetching a package. The colonel never said he had a woman on the way."

Helen shrugged and smiled weakly. "There are my trunks. Could you tell me how best to get to Last Gasp?"

"I'm heading back there. I'll see you there," Slocum said, still not comfortable with his role. He found Helen to be a lovely, courageous woman bearing up well to the bad news he gave her, yet the situation struck him as odd.

Slocum left her sitting and staring into the distance, wrapped in her black thoughts, while he rustled up a buggy and a horse. Within the hour he had her two large trunks loaded into the back and had started on the rough road leading to Last Gasp.

Helen Frederickson stood to one side of the small crowd, dressed in black, dabbing at her eyes with a lace handkerchief. She stared at the grave site, ringed by a low iron fence and notable for its large marble headstone. The stone mason had insisted on working day and night until he finished it. Slocum had to admit he had never seen a finer tribute, even in the Elk, Moose, or Mason cemeteries dotted around the West.

"Hate to trouble you, Mr. Slocum," said the proprietor of the general store, "but we got some supply problems."

"What?" asked Slocum, distracted. He listened to the shopkeeper's dilemma of buying low-cost goods in Santa Fe or more reliable but higher-cost goods from Albuquerque. He watched Helen, and saw how she fought to keep her grief in control. He admired her for that, and wondered what she would consider doing next.

"So, Mr. Slocum?"

"Dealing with Thomasen will be your undoing," Slocum decided. "Get on up to Santa Fe and see what you can do to smooth out the supply problems."

"Good idea. I know the colonel had low regard for Thomasen ever since that coal sale. Should have figured this one out for myself. Thanks." With that the shopkeeper bustled off.

Slocum blinked, realizing he was being asked to solve more and more problems around town. He smiled wryly. After all, he *did* own Last Gasp. Seldom had he felt as at home anywhere as he did here. The people were friendly, and the role of being owner of everything in sight suited him. For the moment.

What worried him more than anything else was how easy it had been to inherit the town. He had been ventilated more than once during his life, a couple of times far worse than the leg and arm wounds while defending Thornton Marks, but never before had he been rewarded so handsomely for it. It made him feel a bit guilty.

"What do you figure she'll do, John?" asked Doc Newton, coming up the road from town.

"She might stay here for a spell, but there's nothing to hold her," Slocum said.

"I hear more in your voice than you're saying. What is it?"

Slocum looked at the doctor. The man had a way of cutting through the fog and finding the target. Slocum shrugged. "I'm about healed up enough to go after the men who killed Marks."

"You're not antsy about that. You have ice water in your veins."

"That a compliment?"

"Just a simple statement of fact. I know what's been

eating at you. It's not sitting around town running things. From the glint in your eye, I'd say you enjoy being in charge. I'd say your problem is that you don't feel you did anything to deserve it all.''

"He must have family somewhere. He was going to marry her."

"The colonel never mentioned anyone else. For all I know, he was an orphan. Go on, ask Miss Frederickson. She might know better than any of us."

Slocum started to say she deserved the bounty from Last Gasp more than he did, then held his tongue. He knew nothing about her other than that she had shown up at the railroad depot claiming to be Colonel Marks's betrothed. Still, Slocum had gone through a lot of poker games sizing up his opponents, knowing when they were bluffing and when they held a decent hand. Everything about Helen Frederickson told him she was truly distraught over the colonel's death and that there wasn't much in the way of phony in her.

"May I escort you back to town?" Slocum asked her.

"Thank you, Mr. Slocum. Seeing the grave is a new shock. I know you had told me he was dead, but I . . . I never really knew him."

"After a dozen years you might not know a person," Slocum said. "It depends on the people." He helped her into the buggy and they rode silently back to the house at the end of town the women of Last Gasp had fixed up for Helen. Slocum paused after he reined back.

"Yes?" she asked.

"I'm staying in the colonel's house. You might go through it and see if there's something you'd like to keep as a memento." Slocum felt helpless while making this offer, and didn't know why.

"Is this proper?" she asked.

"I'm going to be hitting the trail soon. Any time you want to go through the colonel's belongings, feel free.

Anything you want is yours since you are as close to family as he had. I'll tell Ben Longbaugh it will be all right. He's the town banker and was a good friend of Marks.''

"You're leaving Last Gasp?''

"I have to track down the men who killed the colonel,'' Slocum said, a hardness coming on him that hadn't been there before. He had felt a cold rage before that three men would waylay Marks and him. Now, seeing what it meant to Helen Frederickson, the coldness turned to a white-hot anger that wouldn't stop burning until justice had been served.

Six-gun justice.

"You've been so good to me. I hardly know how to thank you.''

"I reckon you might be gone when I get back. It's been good meeting you. I just wish it had been under other circumstances,'' Slocum said.

"I agree.'' Helen averted her bright green eyes and dabbed at new tears forming in the corners. "Would it be too forward of me to suggest dinner together this evening? While the others in town have been nice, you have gone out of your way to put me at ease, Mr. Slocum. Surely, there is a restaurant where we could . . .''

"The wife of the telegrapher puts out a table now and then. I'll see if she can come up with something. It won't be as elegant as I'm sure you are accustomed to, but Mrs. Pond serves a decent meal.''

"Thank you, John,'' she said, putting her hand on his. It felt frail, like a bird's wing, and as fluttery. More than this, it felt cold, as if all life had passed from her.

"I'll have some of the women come by later this afternoon and see how you are getting on,'' he said.

"Thank you,'' Helen said, jumping from the buggy before he could offer to help. She hurried off. From the bow to her shoulders, he realized how heavy the weight of Colonel Marks's death lay on her. He yeehawed, got the horse moving, and left the rig at the stables. He had a dinner to arrange.

Somehow, he felt better than he had since coming to Last Gasp—and worse at the same time, knowing he would soon leave it and Helen Frederickson.

"This is perfectly wonderful," Helen said. The red-and-white checked tablecloth fluttered in the crisp evening breeze. The sun had long since slipped behind the Sandia Mountains to the west, cooling off the entire canyon. The victuals Mrs. Pond had laid out were about the best Slocum had ever tasted.

Or was it the company he kept?

Helen Frederickson looked radiant this evening.

"I would have thought the fancy restaurants would be more to your liking," he said.

"Truthfully, John, I've never eaten at any place better. I am not rich or high society. Thornton knew that. My parents died a few years ago. Cholera. I was a nurse, and took a touch also. My convalescence was long."

"You never married?"

"My fiancé was a navy officer. We were to marry when he returned. He and his ship never did get back. A storm, they said, off the coast of Florida. I was nineteen and idealistic. I refused to believe he was gone."

"So you never found another man to marry?"

Helen smiled wanly. "I devoted myself to being a nurse. The cholera outbreak was devastating to me. My entire family perished. And afterward, the husband of a woman I cared for gave me a letter from a friend of his out West."

"The colonel?"

"Yes," she said softly, her eyes growing distant. She shook herself, reached into her small clutch purse, and drew out a photograph of Thornton Marks. "I suppose

I fell in love with the picture, but our letters told me he was a good man, a decent one.''

''You can tell that by the way everyone in Last Gasp liked him,'' Slocum said. He bit his lower lip, considering turning over the entire town to her. Women couldn't own real property outright, but Ben Longbaugh could see to the day-to-day running of the town. There had to be some way around the letter of the law. Slocum wasn't deserving of the riches here. For all she had been through, Helen warranted more—perhaps even all of Last Gasp.

Before he could broach the subject to her, a ruckus down the street caught his attention.

''What is going on?'' Helen asked, dabbing at her lips with her napkin. ''It looks like those men are beating up the portly fellow.''

''The portly fellow is the town marshal,'' Slocum said. ''Dawkins isn't much of a lawman, but then there's usually not much for him to do in Last Gasp. Excuse me.''

He pushed from the table, reached over to pull the leather thong off the hammer of his six-shooter, then hurried down the street to where two men took turns hitting and kicking Marshal Dawkins.

''John!'' Helen called. He turned to her. ''Be careful! They look like utter thugs!''

He touched the brim of his hat, then went into the middle of the street. He walked quickly, not hurrying, but like an irresistible force of nature sweeping down the dusty street. The two men never paid him a bit of mind. They were having too much fun stomping the marshal.

''Gents,'' Slocum said, ''you might have missed this, but that's the town marshal.''

''We know who this lily-livered coward is,'' said the bigger of the pair. He looked to be off the range, unshaven, shaggy, and wearing trail clothes long since overdue for washing.

"Then you ought to know you shouldn't be planting your boot into his ribs."

"Why not?" the larger of the two began to say. He never finished his sentence. Slocum hauled off and landed a haymaker smack in the middle of his belly. The man folded like a bad poker hand.

Slocum swung around, right hand at his side, fingers slightly curled. He came up on the balls of his feet and bent his knees slightly, facing the other man.

"You want to go for that hogleg, be my guest. Don't figure you'll do anything ever again, though," Slocum said coldly.

"Who are you to go spoilin' our fun?" the man said. His teeth were black and broken. He had the habit of poking his tongue in and out through a gap at the side. Slocum wondered if he ought to shoot him for this show of bad taste alone.

"I'm the man who is going to run you out of town," Slocum said.

"Wait, Slocum, no, don't," Dawkins gasped out from the ground. "I was tryin' to run 'em in. They tried to set fire to the general store, jist for fun. They're dangerous characters."

"Now we have a problem," Slocum said in a level voice. "The marshal wants to lock you up. I want to shoot you where you stand. Which is it going to be?"

"You can't arrest us!" the smaller of the pair said. "You don't dare."

"You're right. I can't arrest you. Only the marshal can do that. But I can—and will—put a bullet through your empty head."

"We're leavin' town," said the smaller one, helping his companion to his feet. "But we'll be back, and you won't like it!"

"I don't much like you being here the first time," Slocum said.

From either side of the street came men, some with rifles in their hands, other fidgeting as if they wanted to have their own guns. They gathered in a circle around Dawkins.

"You need the doc?" asked one. "I can go fetch him."

"I'll be all right," Dawkins said, struggling to his feet. He pushed away the people trying to help him. He came over to Slocum and jutted out his chin, trying to look fierce. "You stay out of my way when I'm trying to bring in criminals. Lettin' 'em go like that will only bring more trouble down on our heads."

With this Slocum had to agree.

6

Marshal Dawkins took a few steps, then fell face-forward into the dust. Slocum was slower to react to the fall than Helen Frederickson. The tall, dark-haired beauty had come to see what was happening. She rushed to kneel by the marshal's side.

"I think he has broken ribs," she said, her strong fingers working along the man's side. "Better get him to the doctor's surgery right away. He might be bleeding inside. And if a lung is punctured . . ." She shrugged.

"You two, help me get him to Doc Newton's," Slocum said, pulling a pair of men from the crowd. Together they got the weakly struggling lawman to the doctor's office. Slocum left Dawkins there, the marshal protesting that he was all right.

"He has broken ribs, doesn't he?" Helen asked Slocum.

"The doc thinks so," Slocum answered. "I'd better arrange to have a couple deputies hired to take his place until he can get back to his job." Slocum wondered if he needed to deputize anyone. Last Gasp wasn't the kind of town where much in the way of lawbreaking occurred. Still, Dawkins had said the two owlhoots who had whupped up on him had threatened to burn the store to the ground. For a while, it wouldn't hurt having a few extra eyes watching.

Slocum talked with Ben Longbaugh a few minutes and approved the money for the deputies, then returned to Helen's side.

"The banker knows a couple cowboys who can fill in for Dawkins till he's mended. I'd better see you home. I don't think those two from before will be back, but I don't want to take any chances."

"I'm not used to such goings-on," Helen said, "but you handled yourself well. I saw how you backed them down."

"I'd've killed them if they hadn't hightailed it," Slocum said. The way she looked at him told him she understood he meant what he said.

"The West is a harsher place than I thought it would be," she said. "Thornton told stories of how rough it was, but . . ."

"It's hard for someone who's not lived out here to know. Still, it's peaceful most of the time. These are good people in Last Gasp. A lot of them have never even picked up a six-shooter."

"You are comfortable with one, though," she said. "Thornton was like you in many ways, I think."

Slocum snorted. "He was a British officer. He was nothing like me. I'm a drifter." Slocum didn't add that he was also wanted for murdering a carpetbagger judge and other crimes too numerous to mention.

"I'm not talking about that. There's a steel center to you that never varies. You are sure what you do is right, honorable, just."

They stopped outside the house where Helen had left her belongings.

"I'm sorry dinner was spoiled," he said. "It seems I'm doing more and more to run this town, even if I don't want to. It'll be a relief in some ways to go after the men who killed the colonel.''

"A man of action, like Thornton," she said. She started to say something more, then stopped. A noise inside the house caught both their attentions.

"Wait here," Slocum said. His six-shooter came easily from its cross-draw holster as he pushed through the door of the darkened house. Moving like a ghost through the rooms, he sought the source of the disturbance. He found it in the small bedroom.

Sitting next to a broken lamp, licking its paws clean of kerosene, was a mangy bobcat. The feline looked up, its tufted ears pointed directly at Slocum. It hissed, pawed in his direction, then jumped to the bed and through the open window in an easy bound.

Slocum shoved his six-gun back into the holster and sat on the bed, letting out a sigh. He looked up to see Helen coming in. She grinned.

"I saw the cat. A lynx?"

"Bobcat hunting for food, I reckon," Slocum said. "It tangled with your lamp." The pungent smell of kerosene was already fading. Only a few drops had been in the lamp.

"I need to remember to close my windows," Helen said, sitting beside him on the bed.

"I intend leaving at first light," Slocum said. "I'd better be . . ."

He stopped, seeing the expression on her face in the moonlight from the window. He knew better than to do it, but he moved closer to kiss her. Her lips parted slightly in invitation. They kissed, almost chastely at first, then with growing passion. Slocum had liked her beauty from the moment she'd set foot on the depot platform in Lamy. In the next couple of days he had come to admire her strength and determination.

Her breasts crushed against his chest as they sank down to the bed.

"We shouldn't do this," he said. "It's not proper."

"It's not," Helen said softly, "but it is what I want. More, it is what I *need*."

Slocum wasn't going to deny her.

They sank back onto the bed, arms wrapped around each other's straining bodies. Slocum was never quite sure how it happened, but Helen managed to work off his gunbelt and boots, and then started on the buttons at his fly. He worked more on kissing her neck and ears than getting off her clothing. Somewhere in the back of his mind a small voice told him this was wrong.

She was a decent woman, not some soiled dove from a dance hall. She was—or had been—the fiancée of a man he respected. It seemed wrong.

But Slocum gave in to temptation. His mind told him making love to Helen was wrong, and his body said it was completely right.

He gasped when she succeeded in freeing him from his jeans. Her hand was warm and firm around his hardness. She stroked up and down gently, stimulating him. He turned into an iron bar in nothing flat.

"I am inexperienced at this," Helen said. "Only once have I—"

"There's no need to tell me your complete history," Slocum said, shutting off her explanation with a deep kiss. His tongue roved into her mouth and dueled with hers. Then he retreated. He was pleased to find that hers followed. Back and forth, their tongues played tag like small children enjoying an afternoon frolic.

Then Helen broke off and stared at him.

"I *have* to tell you. I don't want you thinking I am a loose woman. Before William set sail, we knew we were going to be married. He had proposed, and I had accepted."

"You couldn't bear the thought of him being gone for months?" Slocum guessed.

"That's right. You do understand. John, you're so unlike others I have met."

She squeezed down on his manhood and began stroking. Slocum stiffened even more as he worked from her earlobe to her neck to the deep valley between her fine breasts. His eager mouth pulled and tugged and untied cunning knots holding her frilly undergarment in place. Helen was soon naked to the waist, revealing twin mounds of luscious flesh for him. She had given him a good deal of enjoyment so far.

It was now his turn to give her a similar helping of joy.

Over and around, up and down those snowy white slopes, his tongue raced. He found just the right places to lick and kiss and suck. And then he moved even lower. He thrust his tongue into the deep depression of her navel. He felt her straining like a racehorse in a starting gate, eager and tense and wanting more.

She arched her back, allowing him to pull off the rest of her clothing. She lay in the moonlight from the window, naked and utterly desirable. He looked down at her, then gently ran his hands along the insides of her thighs.

"I'm trembling, John," she said. "This is so good, but—"

"But it is also a big decision. Should we go on?"

She reached up and grabbed him, almost savagely pulling him forward. She kissed with an ardor that took his breath away. There was no mistaking her passion and her need. He moved into the vee formed by her slender white legs. She parted her thighs enough for him to work forward. The tip of his manhood touched the moist gates to her most intimate fastness.

Slowly he advanced, slipping into the tightness until he was hidden full-length.

"This is sheer heaven, John! Paradise! More! Give me everything!"

He began moving, with slow, methodical strokes at first, then building, until he was burning with the friction of their flesh striving, thrusting, moving, turning, and twisting into an erotic explosion.

Helen gasped and clutched at him moments before he felt the fiery tide building deep within his own loins. Locked together, they strove to achieve ecstasy. He could not say about Helen, but seldom had lovemaking been this good for him.

He sank down and lay beside her. She snuggled in the circle of his arms, her head against his chest. For a long while she said nothing.

Then: "Your heart is so strong and even, John. I could lie here listening to it forever."

"You know what I have to do?" he asked.

"Yes," she said, sighing. Her hot breath gusted across his chest. "You might be like William and never return. Or Thornton. It seems I bury my men."

"I've been pretty good at staying alive so far," Slocum said. "I don't intend to let a couple backshooters get the better of me."

"I hope not," she said. He felt a tear rolling onto his chest.

"Who were they, Marshal?" Slocum stared at Dawkins, who was wrapped up in bandages so hardly any flesh showed through. The lawman lay on his narrow bed, taking short gaps rather than normal breaths.

"Don't know which is worse, what they done to me or what the doc did." He tried to sit up, and slumped back, going white with the pain of the broken ribs.

"You know them," Slocum said. "I can tell by the way you talk about them."

"They're part of the gang led by a man called Billy

Dee. Fast gun, he is. Vicious killer. These boys ride with him and think the law means nothing.''

Slocum nodded. Dee's influence extended beyond the city limits of Albuquerque, it seemed.

"You know where they're likely to hole up?''

"One of the canyons nearby. They rob stagecoaches and trains. Dee kills anything that moves.''

"He won't any more,'' Slocum said.

"How's that?'' The marshal looked at him sharply.

"That's why Dee's gang tried to kill the colonel and me. Me in particular,'' Slocum said. His mind raced. Most of those men wouldn't know him. They'd know their boss was dead, but maybe not who had pulled the trigger on him. Slocum tried to remember more about the pair who had gotten away in Albuquerque, and the burly owlhoot who had killed the third in the poker game with Marks.

"You ever tell the colonel about this Dee and his gang?'' Slocum asked.

"He might have knowed,'' Dawkins said. "I saw no reason to bother him with details. Dee left our shipments alone.'' He laughed harshly. "Who'd want to steal coal?''

"What about the payments for the coal?'' Slocum remembered the wad of greenbacks Thomasen had paid over. That much money would draw a man like Billy Dee like a vulture to carrion.

"Mostly kept in a Santa Fe bank. The colonel'd draft against it when he needed. We're pretty self-sufficient out here. Have to be.''

"Well, Billy Dee is dead, and when the bunch from Albuquerque tells those camped out here in the canyon, likely the ones who roughed you up, they might just come looking for me.''

"What you gonna do?'' Dawkins said after working through what Slocum meant. He looked at Slocum with something akin to fear now. The man who'd killed Billy Dee had to be one tough hombre.

"You're all laid up. I had Ben Longbaugh hire a couple of deputies, but the best way of stopping Dee's gang is to find them and cut their hearts out somewhere else." Slocum hitched up his gunbelt and left. Dawkins called out questions Slocum had no desire to answer.

Saddling, after seeing to his provisions and filling his saddlebags with ammunition, Slocum set out to the south, backtracking to the place where he and the colonel had been drygulched. Three from Dee's gang had done the chore there. Only two had left alive. That made Slocum wonder if they'd taken the body of the third man, or maybe put it into a shallow grave somewhere close.

A day of searching brought him to a camp where a half dozen had bivouacked for some time. He could tell by the debris around the camp that they'd had no mind to be tidy. Pawing through the litter, he found a sheet of paper with jagged lines, a crude map showing Tijeras Canyon and a path to the east and north heading up to Apache Canyon where the AT&SF railroad tracks ran.

Slocum hunkered down and studied the map a spell, then decided whoever had taken over from Dee had continued his dead boss's reign of banditry. The gang had planned to rob a train as it slowed for the steep grade through the narrow canyon to the north.

"When?" he wondered. Slocum paced around the camp, determined the outlaws had left only a day or two earlier—and then found the grave behind a salt cedar, halfway downhill toward an arroyo. They hadn't dug deep in the rocky ground, but had used fist-sized stones to cover the body. Already an enterprising coyote had pawed away part of the cairn.

Slocum worked a few minutes, and almost gagged at the odor as he opened the upper end of the grave. He thought he recognized one of the men who had been in the poker game with a drunk Colonel Marks, the one called Mike. That meant he had two lesser owlhoots left, Slim and one other, men with far less courage. That explained why he and the colonel, though wounded severely, had run them off so easily.

Now those two had rejoined the gang. Whoever was in charge was likely as rough and mean as Billy Dee.

Slocum hit the trail, following the crude map through winding canyons until he hit the plains east of the Sandias and then started north toward Apache Canyon, hidden away in the Sangre de Cristo Mountains. He might be too late. Then again, he might be just in time.

7

The sun beat down on him, but Slocum found adequate water along the trail, some in stock tanks and more in small streams running from both the Sandia and Sangre de Cristo Mountains. The rocky patch of prickly-pear-festooned desert quickly turned into rugged, stony foothills as the foothills sloped upward into decent mountains. He picked his way along until he crossed the railroad tracks meandering north and east from Lamy toward distant Kansas City.

It didn't take Slocum very long to find a half-dozen signs that a large band of men, maybe as many as a dozen, had ridden this way within the past few days. Considering how sloppy the Dee gang had been back in Tijeras, Slocum didn't doubt he was following them now straight into the throat of Apache Canyon.

The railroad tracks had been blasted into the side of the mountain. In places, the railroad bed was hardly wider than a wooden tie. Slocum had to pick his way along, knowing the danger if he was in a narrow spot when the train came barreling along.

It was a mighty long fall to the canyon floor.

Horsemen usually traveled along the Santa Fe Trail,

out on the plains where it was flatter and a decent road showed the way. Slocum knew the remnants of the Dee gang weren't likely to choose that path. There might be federal marshals or troopers from nearby Fort Union traveling along it.

He dismounted and led his skittish horse along a particularly narrow stretch. A few man-sized crevices had been blasted into the obdurate rock, hidey-holes for workers to cower in should the train come by and they were unable to get off the tracks. But Slocum saw none large enough for him and his horse. This added speed to his step, even as it seemed to spook his horse.

He emerged from the narrow draw into a space once used to store equipment and encamp the railroad workers. Heaving a sigh of relief, Slocum led his horse off the tracks and into the meadowy area. Barely had he left the tracks when he heard a dull explosion.

It came at him through the ground and up his legs as well as through the air to crash into his eardrums. Quickly following the explosion came the sharp reports of rifles.

"The robbery," he said to himself. Slocum went back to the track, almost having to drag his horse behind him. Dropping to his belly, he put his ear to the steel rail. Vibration told him a train engineer was frantically trying to brake. But how far away along the winding canyon?

"Can't be too much farther," he decided. He pictured what the gang had done. A stick of dynamite had dislodged a rock above the track. The engineer had panicked and thrown on the brakes, sending hot sparks leaping into the dry mountain air. The stench of burning steel and gunpowder had followed as the gang rushed downhill, jumping onto the cars and going for the loot. Money in the strongbox in the mail car? Valuables on the passengers? Both.

From what he had heard of Billy Dee, these men were

as likely to rob everyone and leave them dead as they were to simply take what valuables they could find.

Slocum unlimbered his Winchester and patted his horse on the neck. "You stay here. I won't be long."

Either he stopped them fast or they killed him. Those seemed the only two possibilities. Having the element of surprise on his side counted for a great deal. Slocum didn't intend to let it slip from his grasp.

Hiking fast uphill, he rounded a bend and saw the robbers swinging down off the tops of the railroad cars. Slocum levered a round into the chamber, patted his jacket pocket to assure himself he had plenty of spare ammo, then headed for higher ground. The slope was mostly loose gravel the size of marbles and slippery as hell under his boots. He struggled for several minutes, driving his toes in as if climbing in soft dirt, wincing every time he heard a gunshot in the direction of the train. Were the robbers killing people at random?

Slocum shoved that from his mind. He couldn't do anything about their crimes before he got into position. He got to the top of a low hill, and ran along it until he came to a spot even with the engine. Dropping to his belly, he shoved his rifle in front of him and began hunting for likely targets.

His finger squeezed off a round before he realized he had anyone properly sighted. The outlaw jerked around, dropped to his knees, then fell on his side, spilling a bag laden with coins and jewelry taken from passengers.

"Somebody's shootin' at us!" called a shrill voice. Slocum winged the man complaining.

"All right, whoever you are!" shouted a voice Slocum recognized. The last survivor of the Albuquerque card game came out of the passenger car, his six-shooter shoved into the side of a woman's head. "Throw down your rifle and give up or I'll plug her! I mean it!"

The woman was crying, but seemed game enough for

what Slocum intended. He stood slowly, showing himself. The man with the pistol swung his six-gun around to shoot Slocum.

That was as far as he got. Slocum brought up his rifle and pulled the trigger in a smooth action that sent a slug through the outlaw's face. Death hit long before the owlhoot's trigger finger could respond. The outlaw fell backward, freeing the woman.

"Get on out of here!" went the command. "There's an entire posse on us!"

Slocum fired until the magazine of his rifle came up empty, but failed to wing any of the fleeing train robbers. He skidded down the hillside to where the conductor tried to soothe the woman who had been used as a shield.

"You all right?" Slocum asked.

"I could have been killed!" she cried. "You risked my life!"

"He would have blown your head off and never thought twice about it," Slocum said. She was unharmed. That was good enough. He didn't care if she thought he was a hero or a villain. He had evened the score a little. Seeing the dead bandit up close confirmed his suspicion. It was the one called Slim. But that left a third one, one Slocum did not know, who had ambushed him and Colonel Marks.

"Two down, one to go," he said, trying to remember what the third man from Billy Dee's gang had looked like. It was someone he hadn't seen before or since. Right now, Slocum would have been as happy as a pig in slop to gun down the whole damned gang.

"You a bounty hunter?" asked the conductor.

"This is personal. Three of them killed Colonel Marks from down in Last Gasp. They damned near got me too. Now it's time for them to pay up." Slocum glanced up the slope where the bandits had fled, wondering if he could get in just one more shot.

He started reloading his rifle.

"It'll take us a good hour to clear the track. You can get a ride into Lamy if you want," the conductor promised. "You deserve something for this, and I doubt a reward is in the cards."

"They didn't get what was locked up in your mail car?"

"Nope," the man said, grinning savagely.

That would make the fleeing outlaws angry and maybe just a bit more careless. Slocum started after them, the stones rattling under his boots as he went up the steep embankment above the tracks. He fell flat onto his belly again when he crested the rise, wary that they might have left a rear guard to bushwhack any pursuers.

He saw nothing but emptiness.

Scrambling on, Slocum found their path and where a dozen horses had been tethered. He studied the terrain, took a deep breath of the high mountain air, then started up another steep slope. If he gauged the trail properly, it curled around this mountain and the path led down the far side. He went up and over, trying to erase the lead the robbers had on him.

Sweating like a pig and panting harshly, Slocum topped the hill and saw eight riders several hundred yards below him. They picked their way down the rocky trail carefully, no longer worried about pursuit.

"Guess again," he said quietly. Slocum had been a sniper in the war, and a good one. Dropping so he could rest his hand against a rock and the rifle in the palm of that hand, he picked his target well.

He might get the third man from the end of the procession and cause some agitation. Or he could go for a clean kill.

He sighted in on the last man. His finger came back smoothly and the rifle bucked reassuringly. Slocum knew a good shot, and this felt like one of his best.

The last outlaw flopped backward from the saddle to lie on the rocky trail. Slocum got another round into his chamber, but the robber in front of the downed man had already put his heels to his horse's flanks and gotten out of the line of fire. Slocum had to content himself with one kill.

He made his way down the slope and caught the man's horse. Then he knelt by the man, startled to see he was still alive. Rolling him over, Slocum saw the reason. The man had a half dozen silver dollars in his shirt pocket. Slocum's bullet had drilled through three of them, saving the man's life. An ugly bruise spread out over the man's heart—but he was otherwise unharmed.

The force of the bullet had knocked him out rather than taking his foul life. Slocum stood, muzzle aimed at the man's head. This shot wouldn't miss. For almost a minute Slocum stood, finger curled around the trigger, wondering why he didn't finish the man off.

"Too damned much responsibility in Last Gasp," he decided aloud. It was easy killing the outlaw. Letting him stand trial would be a sight better. "Maybe I can get some information out of him," Slocum said, rationalizing his decision not to kill him outright.

Slinging the man over the saddle, Slocum mounted behind and forced the horse back along the path, arriving in time to see the last of the rock cleared from the tracks.

"You caught one? I'll be switched," the conductor said.

"You got any railroad detectives who might be interested in him?"

"Not in Santa Fe," the conductor said, scratching his head before putting his cap back on. "But the federal marshal's a good man. He might take a hankering to adding to his collection of owlhoots holding up trains."

"My horse is about a half mile down the tracks. Can you pick up my mount?"

"For you, mister, anything." The conductor went off, whistling a jaunty tune. He spoke for several minutes to the engineer, who waved to Slocum, then let out a blast on the whistle.

The ride into Santa Fe took better than two hours, mostly because the engineer was leery of going around the bends too fast. The last time he had done that, he had found a pile of rock and a band of robbers.

"You surely did save us a young fortune, Mr. Slocum," said the depot master at Lamy. "This shipment's been on my mind for a month or more."

"What was in it?"

"Silver coin in bags. Six strongboxes full of scrip destined for Fort Union. And these," the man said, clutching a small brown-paper-wrapped box to his chest as if his life depended on it. Seeing Slocum's curiosity, the man looked around, then opened the parcel with his penknife.

"Don't go tellin' anyone else about this, you hear?" The depot master held out an open box of cigars for Slocum to choose one. The aroma rose and made Slocum's nostrils widen in appreciation. He smoked quirlies when he could get them. Hand-rolled cigarettes when he couldn't. Mostly he went without.

This was a box of cigars worth any one of the bags of coin in the mail car. He took one with real appreciation.

"My brother is down in Havana," said the depot master. "He sent them to his wife, and she sent them to me for my birthday."

"Happy birthday," Slocum said, striking a lucifer and inhaling deeply.

"You made it happier, Mr. Slocum," the man said.

"Not only do I get my cigars, I don't have to explain how the AT&SF lost fifty thousand dollars in coin and payroll."

"The conductor said the federal marshal in Santa Fe might take that owlhoot off my hands." Slocum jerked his thumb in the direction of the trussed-up robber. The man struggled futilely against the ropes Slocum had used to bind him. Many a calf had tried to escape Slocum's clever dogging rope and failed. He didn't think this owlhoot would be any more adept.

"That'd be Jack Slattery. Tough as nails, that one. Just the kind of lawman you want to give his kind to." The depot master glared in the direction of the trussed-up outlaw.

"Thank you kindly," Slocum said. "This is the best reward I could hope for saving your train and its passengers."

The depot master chuckled. "You surely did stir up that woman passenger. She wants your scalp."

"After I finish this smoke," Slocum said, smiling crookedly. He grabbed the end of the rope wrapped around the train robber and pulled hard, getting the man to his feet. "We got some traveling to do before sundown. Let's go."

As they rode from Lamy toward Santa Fe some fifteen miles off, Slocum silently puffed on the cigar until it was nothing but a pleasant memory.

"You can buy a dozen smokes like that if you let me go," the outlaw said, seeing Slocum's satisfaction with the cigar.

"What?"

"Jeff'd pay you big money if you let me go."

"Who's Jeff?" Slocum asked, figuring it had to be the man who had taken over leadership of the Dee gang.

"Jeff Dee, Billy's brother. He's a smart one, smarter

even than Billy. Billy was a crazy killer, but Jeff, now, he uses his head.''

''He plan this robbery?''

''Would have worked if it hadn't been for you,'' the outlaw said glumly.

''Maybe,'' Slocum allowed. ''Where's Dee holed up?''

''You let me go and—'' The man stopped in mid-sentence when Slocum's laughter drowned him out.

''What kind of fool do you think I am?'' Slocum said. ''I let you go, and I wouldn't see anything of you again except your dust—until you drew a bead on the middle of my back some night.''

''We're honorable men. I keep my promises,'' the outlaw said. But Slocum heard the lie in those words. He considered torturing the train robber to find out where Jeff Dee had taken his brother's gang.

As before, when he'd had a chance to end the robber's miserable life, Slocum hesitated. Something about owning Last Gasp did that to him. Or was it only being rich? His thoughts kept drifting back to Helen Frederickson and the send-off she had given him.

''I could buy a dozen boxes of cigars like that,'' Slocum said. ''What do I need money for?''

''You're about the only man I ever heard say that,'' the outlaw replied. ''We could use a man who wanted money and lots of it. I dunno about you, though. Jeff's a good judge of character. Talk to him and maybe you could join up with us, even if you didn't want a cut of our loot.''

Slocum did not respond. The man was either desperate to get away or just plain stupid. He wasn't sure which. Might have been both. The closer they got to Santa Fe the more the man pleaded to be let loose. His rewards soared, as did promise of vile punishment from Jeff Dee should he lose another of his gang.

Through the plaza, past the Palace of the Governors, and beyond the church, Slocum rode with his prisoner. He tugged at the rope and got the man off his horse in front of the hoosegow.

"Looks like you've come to the end of the road," Slocum said. He considered for a moment. "Maybe that's the end of your rope. You wanted for some hanging offense?"

A thrill went through him as he said those words. Did Marshal Slattery hold a wanted poster with Slocum's picture on it too?

"What we got here?" said a gruff voice. A man with a potbelly hanging out over a gunbelt stepped from the shade of the jailhouse. He kept his thumbs tucked into the belt, hands close enough to the twin six-guns so he could clear leather and get off a couple of quick shots in the blink of an eye.

Slocum wondered if the man actually used both six-shooters or if this was an affectation.

"I'm as good with my left as I am with my right," the marshal said, answering Slocum's unspoken question. "More 'n one road agent's found that out, to his sorrow."

"Snared this one robbing the train," Slocum said. He explained what had happened, then handed over the map he had found.

"You say this one killed Colonel Marks?" Slattery eyed the prisoner with a jaundiced eye.

"Not him. One of those still riding with the Dee gang. I'll know him when I see him."

"You're Slocum, ain't ya?"

"How'd you know?" Slocum tried to keep his hand from a betraying twitch and move toward his Colt Navy.

"Word gets around. You own Last Gasp now. That makes you a man to be reckoned with."

"*This* makes me a man to be reckoned with," Slocum

said, putting his hand on the ebony butt of his six-shooter.

"You'll learn which is more powerful, bullets or bucks," said the marshal. "If you live that long. It was a fool thing going after the Dee gang by your lonesome. Get on into the office. We got papers to fill out on this one."

Slocum shoved the outlaw into the jailhouse and followed. If Slattery had wanted to take him, out in the street would have been the likely spot. The heavyset lawman dropped into a protesting desk chair, grabbed a handful of wanted posters, and leafed through them as if they were a deck of cards. He cut one out and let it flutter to the desktop for Slocum to see.

"That's the gent you brought in. Worth a hundred dollars, he is."

Slocum scanned the list of charges. Leroy Larson had broken out of Detroit Federal Prison, was wanted on charges of robbery and mayhem in four different locales, and was wanted for questioning in the murder of a federal officer in Denver.

"Busy man, Larson," said the marshal. He unlocked a desk drawer and pulled out a lockbox. Another small key opened it. He peeled off five twenty-dollar bills and shoved them across the desk to Slocum. "As if you need 'em," the marshal said.

"If you find out where the Dee gang might be headed, I'd appreciate knowing, Marshal," said Slocum.

"You got the power now, Mr. Slocum. I'll let you know. Just don't go doin' anything too stupid, you hear?"

Slocum scooped up the money, shot a last glance at Larson and wondered if he might have broken and told about Dee's whereabouts, then pushed aside such idle speculation. He had done what he'd done. He was a law-abiding citizen now. A pillar of his community.

The owner of a community.

As Slocum rode out of Santa Fe he saw the large church again. It had a prominent spire and bell tower. The Cathedral of St. Francis of Assisi. He reined back, considered his good fortune, then dismounted and went into the church.

The poor box in the vestibule looked mighty empty. It had a hundred dollars in it, five twenties wrinkled and sweaty from the short time spent in a shirt pocket, after Slocum left.

8

Slocum returned to Last Gasp with anticipation. Curiously, it was also mixed with some trepidation. He had become the real town mayor, giving advice and telling how things should run. He enjoyed the power, and at the same time distrusted it. He had never been in such a position before with so many people looking up to him. During the war he had been a captain, but that was entirely different.

Men had relied on him for their lives, but now they were also worrying about trivial matters, from the next hoedown to finding enough sugar to feed the town's sweet tooth. Coal shipments had to be managed and payrolls met. Slocum had spent more time in a week pushing a pen than he had in the prior year.

They depended on him and his advice. And they shouldn't. They ought to do for themselves.

"I own the town," he muttered. The burden of such riches weighed down on him.

Along with it came the need to see Helen Frederickson again. He was almost afraid she might have left, returning to the East. If she had, he could not blame her. Last Gasp was a rough town, short on luxuries, for all the civilizing effect Colonel Marks had had on the area.

Slocum's eyes fixed on the end of the road as his horse slowly walked, anxious to be back. He had myriad decisions to make, but seeing Helen again would ease that somewhat. The idea kept dancing in his head that he ought to give her a part of the town. He had been at the right place at the right time for Colonel Marks to deed over everything to him on his deathbed. If Helen had been there she would have gotten it all.

Slocum felt he owed her, and didn't know why.

"Guilt," he finally decided after another mile passed under his horse's hooves. The gelding looked back at him, a large brown eye fixed on him. "That's all it is. I feel guilty I didn't do more to save the colonel. She was his wife-to-be, and I robbed her of his company." Slocum pulled the cork from his canteen, took a deep drink, then swallowed. "And I feel like I robbed her of the money that would have come her way because of the colonel's wealth."

That settled in his mind, Slocum considered what he ought to do. By the time he reached the edge of Last Gasp, it was sundown and he had decided that deeding over the town to her was the only proper thing since the colonel didn't have any family. Slocum wasn't cut out to be mayor—and owner—of so much. It tied him down. What happened if he took it into his head simply to ride out one day? What would the people do then?

This was better, letting Helen take over the day-to-day running of Last Gasp. He could get enough money from the bank to see him anywhere he wanted to go. Since he'd ridden up from the south, heading north appealed most to him. Maybe he could take a look around South Pass again. It had been years since he had seen the break in the Rockies that allowed settlers to travel along the Oregon Trail.

Or Denver. It was a booming town now, fed by the

gold and silver fields on the other side of the Front Range. He could find more than one saloon around Larrimer Square with a good poker game in it.

He snorted. Last Gasp didn't even have a decent watering hole. No saloon, and certainly no dance hall with painted women and rotgut so vile it took the paint off wood.

As he rode down the center of the single street in Last Gasp, Slocum noted how quiet the place was. Then he saw rifle barrels thrust through half-closed windows and eyes watching him. Frowning, he reined back in front of the bank. It had closed an hour earlier, but lights still burned inside, telling him Ben Longbaugh worked late as usual.

Rapping on the door brought a furtive shuffle of feet from inside. Longbaugh peered out, a six-gun in his hand. The look of relief when he saw who was there put Slocum on his guard. The door creaked open. Slocum saw how it had been hastily patched. Sometime earlier it had been knocked off its hinges, maybe by a powerful kick.

"What's wrong with everyone?" asked Slocum. "All I saw riding in are rifles and suspicious stares."

Ben looked around outside, then pulled Slocum in and closed the door. He barred it before speaking.

"This afternoon, late. They said it was the Billy Dee gang."

"Billy Dee is dead," Slocum said coldly.

"His brother's in charge of it now. And you done something to rile them up."

"Stopped them from robbing the AT&SF in Apache Canyon. Saved the government a heap of woe and a lost payroll for Fort Union. And I killed two of them and captured another. Took him to Marshal Slattery in Santa Fe."

"They shot up the town like there was no tomorrow,"

Ben said. "Wounded two and, uh, killed two others. The deputies you had me hire."

"What about Dawkins?"

"He's still laid up. Doc Newton says it'll be another week before he can even get out of bed, and maybe a month before he can ride." Ben Longbaugh licked his lips and turned from Slocum.

"What else?" demanded Slocum. "You're keeping something back."

"They hate you bad, John. I could tell from what they said and did. Turning their friend in to the marshal was only part of it. I think they know you killed Billy Dee."

"If the whole gang of them hurrahed Last Gasp, that'll make it easy for me to track them. One or two might hide their trail, but they're so sloppy a half dozen or more never could." Slocum fell silent. The only sound in the bank was the tick-tick-tick of the huge clock on the back wall by the vault.

"What else aren't you telling me?"

"They want you to chase them, John. They did nothing to hide their trail. Quite the contrary. I suspect they left a trail a blind man could follow."

"Then they'll get their wish. I'll be after them at first light." Slocum could do with putting a few more slugs in their worthless hides. He still had the last man to go, the one who had whined the loudest back in Albuquerque. With the other two he had plugged, the colonel's killers would be brought to a proper end.

"They did something to make sure you trailed them." Ben Longbaugh swallowed hard. "John, they kidnapped Helen Frederickson."

Slocum wondered why he felt nothing. Anger? Outrage? Nothing. He just stood and stared at the banker.

"They said you could have her back when you tracked them down."

"She's probably dead by now, or worse," Slocum

said. He realized it was shock that deadened his emotions. "If the two deputies are dead and Dawkins is still stove up, how many others do you think would come with me in a posse?"

"John, I don't know. I simply don't know. The people of Last Gasp might be at the end of their rope. After the Dee gang shot up the town, some actually packed and left. They came here to get away from such things."

"Left?" This surprised Slocum. Their hightailing it so fast startled him. "How many?"

"A dozen, maybe more. They said there was nothing keeping them here. After all, *you* own purty near everything. They're all sharecroppers, so to speak."

"Keep things running the best you can," Slocum said, pulling back the locking bar on the bank door. He glanced again at the splintered wood.

"They kicked in the door, but couldn't open the vault since I was up at the Black Beauty mine seeing about a new shaft they were sinking," Ben said. "Most of the money's safe. All we lost was what was in the tellers' cages."

"I'll get it back. All of it, with interest," Slocum vowed. He slid into the cool night air, the crisp breeze whipping up the canyon to wipe away any sweat on his forehead.

Slocum walked out into the middle of the street and turned slowly. He had the feeling everyone was staring at him. He paused for effect, then called loudly, "Two deputies dead! Robberies! Miss Frederickson kidnapped! I *will not* tolerate this! I want a posse to hunt down those owlhoots! Who's with me?"

Slocum turned slowly again. Windows snapped closed. Doors creaked shut. And the people of Last Gasp prepared to cower the rest of the night, worried that the Dee gang would come back and do to them what had

already been done to the deputies and Helen Frederickson.

Slocum returned to the front of the bank, caught up
the reins of his horse, and led the exhausted animal to
the stable. He curried the horse and made sure enough
grain was within easy reach. The gelding was almost too
tired to appreciate this unexpected bounty.

"Rest up," Slocum said. "We head out at dawn."
His hand went to his six-shooter and drew the Colt. He
broke it open and checked the cylinder. All full. He usually rode with the hammer on an empty chamber. Not
now, not when he might need a full six rounds to end
one vile life after another.

Slocum threw himself into a haystack at the far end
of the stalls and fell asleep within minutes. He slept
heavily, his dreams turning to nightmares of ambushes
and dying colonels and screaming Helens. When he
awoke an hour before sunrise, he was less rested than
when he had lain down.

The dust hung in the air and made him sneeze. Slocum stretched tired muscles, then went for his gun. A
small unexpected sound brought him around, gun drawn
and aimed squarely at the diminutive man standing silhouetted in the doorway. Shadow moved across shadow,
but froze when Slocum cocked the Colt Navy.

"Who's there?" said the high-pitched voice.

"That's my question," Slocum called. "What are you
doing in here?"

"I came to get my horse. The sorrel, down at the far
stall." The man stepped forward so his face was half-
revealed in the pale yellow light of a kerosene lamp
hanging high in the stable. For an instant Slocum
thought he recognized the man, then knew he had never
seen him before.

He looked only fifteen or sixteen, but carried himself
older. He might have been as old as twenty from the

way he looked. Weathered and trail-tanned, he had seen more than a few summers in the hot New Mexico sun. He was cocky, but not the kind of cocky that went with inexperience. Slocum knew only one way of getting such confidence—and that was surviving.

"Do I know you?" Slocum asked. "You look familiar."

"A lot of people say that. Got that kind of face." The man smiled. "My name's . . . Jonesy."

Slocum knew this was a lie from the way the man hesitated before answering. He shrugged this off. Many men used summer names, not caring for their real ones to get around.

"Slocum."

"Pleased to make your acquaintance." Jonesy ambled around. Slocum caught sight of the six-shooter hanging at the young man's hip. It had seen hard use but was well cared for. Jonesy turned to face Slocum squarely. "You gonna shoot me or can I ask you to put that hog-leg away?"

Slocum let the hammer down easy on his six-shooter and returned it to his holster. "Sorry about that. Since yesterday's hurrahing, I've been a little on edge."

"You were here?" Jonesy seemed surprised, but tried to hide it.

"Got in afterward and heard about the trouble. I was up in Santa Fe."

"Nice town, Santa Fe. Business?"

"You might say that," Slocum said. He had thrown down on this stranger and owed him some explanation, but not a full story of his life. "I'm on my way after the Dee gang."

"I was here while they were shooting up the town. Dangerous crowd, that bunch. Heard tell Jeff Dee's the worst of them all now. Been on a tear since his brother was murdered over in Albuquerque."

Slocum didn't bother correcting the young man. What he thought didn't amount to a hill of beans.

"I'm after them when it gets light," Slocum said.

"You a bounty hunter? I bet a gang like that's got a lot of rewards riding on their heads."

"Who knows?" said Slocum. "I might make a few dollars on this. They've been running wild long enough. About time someone brought them to justice."

"You have the look of a man who prefers living on the wrong side of the law," Jonesy said, eyeing Slocum closely. "Don't think a sheriff's badge has ever been pinned on that coat." He moved closer and ran his hand over the left side.

Slocum grabbed the man's wrist and twisted, sending him staggering. Jonesy swung back, fire in his eyes and his lips pulled back in a feral snarl.

"Don't touch me," Slocum said in a tone that stopped the other man dead in his tracks.

"Sorry. Didn't know it was something you were touchy about."

For a long moment neither moved. Then Slocum saw the other man backing down, and the possibility of gunplay passed.

"You getting up a posse?" asked Jonesy. "Or don't you want to split the reward money?"

"Can't find anyone stupid enough to ride along. Doesn't matter much," Slocum said. "Might just slow me down."

"Think there's going to be gunplay?" asked the young man, his voice rising to a shriller level as the possibility of action aroused him.

"Probably," Slocum answered.

"I'd like to go along, if that's all right with you. I'm a fair tracker and you might need a spare gun when the lead starts flying."

"You looking for a deputy's salary or is it only the

reward money?'' Slocum studied the young man carefully. He had long dishwater-blond hair pulled back and held in place by a too-small black Stetson. It rode on the top of his head like some prairie dog poking up out of his hole.

''Adventure,'' the man said quickly. ''It's been too dull for me the past few weeks. Finally, this is a chance to do something that will be worth telling my grandchildren about.''

''Grandchildren,'' snorted Slocum. ''You have any children?''

''No.''

''First things first. Remember that when we finally get on their trail,'' said Slocum.

Jonesy grinned crookedly and went to saddle his horse.

9

"Sloppy work on their part," Jonesy commented, pointing to a campsite where the kidnappers had stopped to brew a pot of coffee. "They didn't even try to hide their trail."

"They want me to find them," Slocum said, dismounting to poke through the ashes left from the fire. Some embers were warm enough to sting his fingers as he sifted through them. The coffee aroma still hung in the crisp mountain air, pungent enough to make his mouth water. He had refused to take time to do more than rest the horses since leaving Last Gasp. A pot of coffee would go well.

"So you can pay the ransom?" asked the young man. He sat with one leg curled around the front of his pommel, leaning forward slightly.

"You might say that." Slocum knew the price the gang wanted for Helen Frederickson. If he didn't rescue her, she would be killed. Even if he found them, she might already be dead. That would be one more score he had to settle with them—all of them.

"Seems like you ought to get the marshal over in Albuquerque to help hunt for this little filly of yours."

"She's not my filly," Slocum said coldly. "She was Colonel Marks's fiancée. She arrived about the time we were planting him in the ground."

"Pity."

"Two of the men who killed Marks are dead. The remaining one will pay soon enough," Slocum said, deciding the trail couldn't be more than a few hours old. Three at the outside. That meant they had to ride more carefully to avoid falling into an ambush. He didn't count Billy Dee's brother as being all that smart, but a cunning animal often proved the most dangerous.

"You carry a powerful grudge, don't you?"

"I promised the colonel I'd see justice done."

"But you didn't get the law in on this? Why not?"

"It'd take too long," Slocum said, tiring of the young man's incessant questions. He made a quick circuit around the camp and saw where they had tied Helen. A piece of fabric from her gingham dress had torn off on a blackberry bush. Slocum knew Jonesy watched him like a hawk as he tugged at the scrap of fabric and pulled it free.

"No question we're on the right trail, is there?" asked the young man.

Slocum silently mounted, his mind stretching ahead to how the fight might play out. Alone, he stood a small chance of rescuing Helen. With Jonesy to provide a diversion, he knew he could do it. Everything the Dee gang did showed how sloppy they were. They would be overconfident, thinking they had the advantage as long as Helen was a prisoner.

He had to turn the tables. Fast.

Slocum put his heels to his tired horse's flanks. Jonesy kept up, his horse straining a mite in the high altitude.

"This here's the pass. Yonder is Albuquerque," Jonesy said, as if lecturing a schoolhouse full of children. "To the east is nothing but the most godforsaken land you've ever seen until you reach the Llano Estacado, which is even more desolate. South is Lincoln County.'' Something in the way he said the name caused Slocum to turn around and stare at him. A look approaching rapture lit the man's face.

''You part of the Lincoln County War?''

''Wish I had been,'' he said. ''Those were fine times. A man could ride and be a man. Not like now. Too danged quiet.''

''You call the Dee gang holding up trains, kidnapping innocent women, and killing men quiet?'' Slocum snorted in disgust. Some folks never knew when they had it good.

''You like a bit of excitement. I can tell. You look like a gunfighter to me. You ever killed a man? Bet you have.''

''I was in the war,'' was all Slocum said. Jonesy rattled on inanely. Slocum ignored what he said, preferring to watch the terrain closely for any hint of ambush.

''This here's Fourth of July Canyon,'' Jonesy announced. ''Purtiest sight you ever seen about this time of year. Oak trees turn beautiful, spaced out among the aspen.''

The canyon stretched down into another range of mountains, distinct from the Sandias. Manzano Mountains, Slocum had heard them called. The Spanish explorers in these parts had had a fascination with naming every pile of rocks they found after red things.

Before Slocum finished with the Dee gang, the ground would soak up gallons of bright red outlaw blood.

''There,'' called Jonesy. ''They cut off the main trail and headed up into this side canyon.''

Slocum nodded. He had already spotted the deviation from the trail. It surprised him the young man picked up the change of direction so fast. Jonesy had not been doing too good a job identifying spoor along the trail, in spite of the sloppy trail left by the kidnappers.

"Why are they heading up there?" asked Slocum, thinking out loud. He took off his Stetson and wiped sweat from his face. The canyon was close and hot. In another few hours it would be getting dark. That might be the best time to attack, if he could find the camp before then.

"You reckon the lady's still alive?"

"She was back when they stopped for coffee," Slocum said. "I haven't seen any sign they stopped to kill her. Haven't even noticed any rider breaking off from the main group. This is the first time they even tried to disguise their trail."

"Maybe they want us to keep riding—into a trap," Jonesy suggested.

"Might be," Slocum said, eyeing the track. How far ahead of them was the gang. And Helen?

Slocum swung off the main trail and followed the small path through a thicket and into a stand of trees. Here the trail showed more clearly. Slocum dismounted and went on foot, more to have the shield of a horse on one side than to follow the trail. Like the rest of their flight to the south from Last Gasp, the gang had not done a good job disguising their spoor.

"This is it?" asked Jonesy, dismounting. He nervously drew his six-shooter and shoved it back into the holster a few times, as if making sure it slid easily against the smooth leather.

"How much experience you have in gunfights?" Slocum asked.

"What?"

"You ever kill a man? Aim a six-gun at him and pull the trigger?" Slocum watched Jonesy carefully. A hint of dark anger clouded the young man's face.

"You calling me a coward?"

"Just asking, if you have to use that six-gun, if there's

going to be any hesitation about snuffing out a man's life.''

"These are scum," Jonesy said hotly. "Why should I have any trouble killing them?"

"Might make a reputation," Slocum allowed, wondering if that was what drove the young man. "You need to be able to keep from shooting if that's what's called for."

"I know when to stir it up and when to watch," Jonesy said. "I'm no greenhorn. I've been in shootouts before."

"Where?"

"I have. Let it lie, Slocum."

Jonesy's tone gave Slocum pause. The youngster was mighty reticent about his past. Slocum couldn't decide if Jonesy was boasting and had never shot it out before, with his life and other lives on the line, or if he might have a reward on his head. The way he'd prodded Slocum about getting the law involved might have been a way of figuring out if he ought to slip off or keep riding with him.

Slocum had no problem with Jonesy's face on a wanted poster. His own had shown up one more than one. What he worried about more was the youth lying. Nothing would be worse than needing an extra gun to back him up and then finding Jonesy had frozen or even turned and run.

"I won't fail you," Jonesy said, as if reading Slocum's mind.

"We're not far from their camp."

"How can you tell?"

Slocum put his finger to his lips. He inhaled deeply and caught the scent of burning juniper and fresh coffee. The gang drank more coffee than anybody he had ever seen, except for a cavalry troop. Right now, he wished the Dee gang had boozed it up in celebration. Tackling a half-dozen drunk outlaws would be easier than shooting it out with sober, cold-blooded killers.

Moving closer, Slocum whispered, "They're ahead of us. Camped. I want you to circle and come on them from uphill. If they have sentries out, get rid of them as quietly as possible. Then you create a fuss and I'll do the rest."

"How do you know they are nearby?"

Slocum wondered if the young man's nose was all stopped up, or if he simply didn't know how to pick up a scent on the evening wind.

"I just know. Not more than a mile from here. Less, I'd say."

"Less," murmured Jonesy. "Got it. So I ride out that way, get around, and come at them from the west?"

"If you can't get between them and the far end of this canyon, hit them from whatever spot looks best. It'd be helpful if we caught them between us. You shoot up their camp and draw their attention."

"Then you rescue the fair maiden," Jonesy finished with an ironic twist to his lip. "You need a white horse, Slocum."

"We won't take them all on, unless it looks like we can finish them. Rescue Miss Frederickson. Then we can decide later how to wrap up their thieving careers."

"You have any spare ammo? All I brought is in my pistol and rifle," Jonesy said.

Slocum fumbled in his saddlebags and brought out a box of ammo for the man's rifle.

"Don't use it all unless you have to. We might need to fight our way back up Tijeras Canyon."

"Good plan," Jonesy said, hefting the box of ammunition. "This might turn into real fun," he said, grinning savagely.

"Let's hope it goes smooth," Slocum said. He'd had a bellyful of killing. If necessary, his six-shooter would speak with its deadly leaden voice, but more and more, Slocum wanted nothing but a little peace in his life.

"Smooth as silk," agreed Jonesy. "How long are you giving me before you move in?"

"An hour," Slocum decided. He guessed the gang's camp was only a few hundred yards away. If Jonesy swung wide and circled, an hour would bring him to a spot where the kidnappers could be driven back down the canyon. A single mistake on the part of any of the gang would spell their end.

He had to be sure any such mistake did not also take Helen with it.

Slocum looped the reins around a tree, letting his horse chew contentedly on a patch of fresh blue grama. He checked his Winchester and then his Colt to be sure he had enough firepower to do the job. He faced six or eight outlaws. Maybe more. With surprise on his side, he could take several of them. With Jonesy taking out one or two, Slocum thought there might be a chance to eliminate the Dee gang entirely.

It might horrify Helen, but it would simplify life in Last Gasp.

"Gallons of blood," Slocum muttered to himself as he silently made his way through the growing twilight. He stepped carefully to avoid dried branches. Even a careless sentry might hear if he grew too slipshod in his own advance on the camp.

Slocum pressed his back against a gnarled pine, bent by the incessant wind blowing down the narrow canyon. He used the rifle barrel to push aside a low-hanging limb and peered into the outlaw camp. Slocum stood motionless for several minutes, studying the lay of the land, finding where each of the gang had laid out his gear— and hunting for Helen.

He couldn't tell, but a tight group of four trees at the far side of the camp seemed the most likely place for them to have tied Helen up. Slocum checked his watch. Twenty minutes had passed. Jonesy wouldn't create his ruckus for another forty.

The temptation burned in him to skirt the camp and go to the stand of trees to rescue Helen right away. Four outlaws lounged on their bedrolls, joking and swapping lies. Two smoked. Slocum's nose wrinkled at the pungent odor of tobacco mingling with the coffee and juniper aromas from the fire. They were fools. They had to know he was on their trail, yet they made no effort to disguise their camp.

"Four in the camp. Maybe that many more scattered around?" Slocum doubted Jeff Dee would have posted four guards. They had been too scornful of others before. He doubted they would change now.

But they had to know he would come after Helen. Soon.

"A trap?" Slocum wondered, staring at the screen of brush around the distant trees. Did they think to lure him into a trap there? He continued studying the camp for another ten minutes. Two more of the gang returned. One had bagged a rabbit. The other had been taking a leak and was buttoning his fly.

Six. How many were left? Slocum wished he knew. Were they standing guard over Helen? He got itchy about that grove of trees. She had to be there. Right?

"Too easy," Slocum decided. They might have two guards posted. But why put both of them up the canyon when they expected Slocum to come from the trail? He had expected to see sentries alert for him on their heels. Since he hadn't, Slocum grew increasingly suspicious of what *had* to be a trap set for him.

Where was the bait? Where were the steel jaws set to clamp shut around his leg? The noose to be dropped around his neck?

Slipping to his belly, Slocum worked his way slowly

away from the trees where he suspected Helen was held prisoner. Within minutes he was glad he had chosen to do more surveillance. He spotted a dark figure, securely bound to a tree trunk just outside the camp and well away from the trees.

It *had* been a trap!

Slocum worked slowly now, taking his time. There would be guards over the kidnapped woman. He reached behind and found the thick-bladed knife sheathed at the small of his back. Indian-style he could take out the guards and maybe escape with Helen before they even knew he was in the vicinity.

That left Jonesy swinging in the wind if he mounted his attack without Slocum to back him up, but if Slocum worked fast he could get Helen back to the horse and on her way to Last Gasp. He could then add his firepower to Jonesy's and eliminate the bunch of owlhoots once and for all.

Slocum wormed his way through the forest floor faster now, making more noise but needing to reach Helen before Jonesy started his attack. She had to be clear of the battlefield so a stray bullet wouldn't injure her—or worse.

As much as he felt the need to hurry, Slocum slowed and finally stopped, lying in the mulch and trying to figure out what was wrong. He could see the woman more clearly now. She was pale and drawn, her face set in a grim mask to hide the fear. Ropes held her wrists behind the rough pine tree, as well as binding her feet securely. One of the gang had taken her scarf and used it to circle her neck and then fastened it behind the tree. She was effectively held immobile. Slocum couldn't tell if they had gagged her.

"Where are the guards?" he wondered. She was securely tied, but if this was intended to be a trap, he figured a couple of the gang ought to be on lookout.

Slocum studied the tree limbs above. No sign of movement save for a lone owl stirring in the twilight, getting ready to hunt a dinner of field mice. Nowhere around did he spot a guard. Slocum doubted any of the Dee gang could hold still longer than a few minutes. He waited and watched patiently for any betraying movement in the undergrowth around Helen.

Nothing.

He had to believe they were stupid enough to think it would take longer for him to catch up with them than he had taken. Slocum worked forward carefully, rifle across his arms. A few rustling sounds betrayed him to Helen, but she could not turn. He saw they had used a piece of rough twine to gag her, the string pulled taut against the corners of her mouth and then fastened around the tree as well. She could hardly move, much less speak.

"Helen, it's me, Slocum," he whispered. He moved closer. "Can you move your head, even a little?"

A faint jerk yes.

"Are there any more of them around?"

A frantic nod yes.

"On guard?"

A shake of the head.

"I'm going to get you free," he said, moving so he had the tree where she was bound between him and the camp. Helen struggled futilely against her ropes.

"Don't," he cautioned. "You'll hurt yourself. There aren't any guards out here."

She tried to turn. Thin ribbons of blood ran from the corners of her mouth as she tried to speak.

"Seems the little lady is trying to warn you about something, Slocum."

The loud cocking sound froze Slocum in his tracks.

"Go on, turn around. Real slow-like."

He turned to face Jonesy's leveled rifle.

"Let me do some proper introductions. I'm Jeff Dee. And you, you son of a bitch, are the one who murdered my brother!"

10

"Yes, sir, Slocum, had you fooled from the very first," chortled Jeff Dee. He pranced around like a banty rooster guarding his flock. He stopped and shoved his face close to Slocum's. Then he spat.

Slocum recoiled slightly, then froze. Anger served no purpose now. He had to get free before wrath would mean anything. He shook his head to get the spittle off his cheek. The men holding him gave no chance to fight his way free.

As sloppy as they had been reaching their campsite, they showed no sign of letting their vigilance slacken for even a second now. Slocum guessed their new leader would kill them if they let their prisoner get free. Jeff Dee strutted back and forth, thumbs tucked into his gunbelt.

"I could have killed you anywhere along the trail," he boasted. "Anywhere, anytime!"

"I did ride so my back was to you," Slocum admitted. "Are you like your brother? Only shoot a man when his back's turned? Or are you any good with that six-shooter?"

Jeff Dee drew and cocked his six-gun with blinding

speed. Slocum never flinched when the young man thrust it into his face.

"So you can draw against an unarmed man," Slocum sneered. "There's a difference when you face someone who can shoot back. Your good-for-nothing brother found that out the hard way." Slocum wanted to goad Dee into a mistake. He might also goad him into pulling the trigger of the pistol shoved between his eyes.

"You got a lot of gall, Slocum. I ought to spill it all over the mountainside."

"Want me to turn around?"

Jeff Dee brought the six-shooter up and down in a short arc that ended on the side of Slocum's head. He sagged in the grip of the men holding him. Pain lanced into his skull and filled his entire body. The old injuries seemed to resonate in sympathy with the new wound, and Slocum couldn't focus his eyes. Blood ran down his cheek from the wound high on his temple.

Slocum's cold eyes eventually fixed on the furious man and seemed to frighten him. Jeff Dee backed off, the six-shooter wavering now. He couldn't decide what to do.

"I caught you fair and square, Slocum. Admit it. I fooled you. You didn't have any idea you were riding with the famous Billy Dee's brother!"

"What would you have done if I had decided to let the marshal over in Albuquerque know you'd kidnapped a helpless woman?"

"You are a piece of work, Slocum, I'll give you that. You'd a been dead in a heartbeat. I like it better this way. This way, we can have some fun with you." Jeff Dee turned and looked back to the tree where Helen struggled against her bonds. "And then we can have a lot of fun with *her*."

Slocum knew Dee was taunting him to produce an angry reaction. He didn't give him the satisfaction.

"Truss him up and put him over there by yonder tree, Clement," Jeff Dee ordered one of his henchman. The one holding Slocum's right arm moved first. Slocum pegged him as the one back in Albuquerque who had killed Zeke. Slocum figured he ought to know the names of the men he killed. A weaselly-faced man whom Slocum now recognized as the third bushwhacker who had helped murder Colonel Marks, stood to one side, looking frightened. Slocum couldn't tell if he was afraid of him or Jeff Dee.

Stout ropes circled Slocum's arms and bound his wrists behind his back. The men spun him around and then shoved him against a sapling. His weight caused it to bend slightly. Clement jerked hard on the rope fastened around Slocum's wrists and pulled him erect again.

"Stand and take this like a man," ordered the outlaw. He smiled, revealing two broken teeth. "If you got any manhood in you."

With that jeer, he retraced his steps to stand beside Jeff Dee. The young man practiced his draw a few times until he seemed satisfied.

"Put a can on Slocum's head," he ordered. With his left hand he grabbed a bottle of whiskey and took a long pull. Wiping his mouth on his sleeve, Dee squared his stance and tried to look tough. He drew and fired.

Slocum jumped as the can flew off his head. Sharp bits of the can cut his forehead.

"I got one. Your turn, Henley." Jeff Dee motioned to the weasel-faced man with whom Slocum had yet to settle the score of Colonel Marks's death. "Here. Take a swig first. It'll steady your nerves."

"I dunno, Jeff. This—"

"Do it."

Henley drank the whiskey, coughed and spat, then drew his six-shooter. He was no gunslinger; Slocum saw that in the way he moved. He just hoped Henley was a good shot.

Another can flew from his head, replaced with another. Then it was Clement's turn.

By the time the entire gang had taken turns shooting cans off Slocum's head, an entire bottle of whiskey had been downed. Jeff Dee walked over, a slight stagger in his gait, and put the empty whiskey bottle on Slocum's head.

"Don't you go flinching none now, you hear?" the gang leader said. "Break out another bottle for me!"

He went back to the campfire and drank heavily. Then he settled down and fired. His first shot missed the bottle entirely. The second slammed into Slocum's left arm, about where he had taken the bullet earlier when the colonel had been killed. The third slug shattered the glass bottle, sending fragments down to slash at Slocum's face.

A tiny river of whiskey burned the cuts as it matted his hair.

"Who's next?" cried Jeff Dee. He staggered around, firing his six-shooter into the air and whooping it up. Before anyone could claim the next shot at Slocum, Dee staggered over and thrust his face up into Slocum's.

"We're a real gang. Billy showed us how to do it. We're gonna ride into Albuquerque," he said, hiccuping, "and we're gonna hurrah the whole damn town. Blow the safe in that two-bit bank, steal every dime from the railroad depot office, then we're gonna turn the town into nothing but splinters and bullet holes. Ain't that right, men?"

They all fired their six-shooters into the air in response. This started a round of boasting. Each outlaw had a more outrageous crime he wanted to commit.

"Every last train comin' into Lamy," Clement declared. "All ours. Every ounce of bullion, every scrap of money. We're gonna roll in greenbacks!''

"Why stop with Albuquerque and that damn train?'' roared Henley, getting into the spirit of the swaggering about and boasting. "Why not hurrah the whole territory! We can do it. Start south and work north. Not even Billy the Kid did anything like that! No lawmen kin stop us!''

"They can't stop us because we're the Jeff Dee gang!'' cried Dee. "We're gonna rob and kill because of what *he* did to Billy.''

With the quicksilver swiftness of a drunk, Dee changed from bragging to downright deadly. He stumbled toward Slocum and cocked his six-gun. This time the barrel rested coldly between Slocum's eyes.

Slocum stared past the barrel to Dee's trigger finger. It turned white and then pulled all the way back with a dull click. The hammer fell on a spent chamber.

Dee fell back and sat heavily on the ground. For a moment, he seemed confused. Then he broke out laughing.

"Get our guest all tied up for the night." He stared at Slocum. "We're not gonna just shoot up Albuquerque and Santa Fe, you know. We're gonna burn Last Gasp to the ground. Every last man, woman, and urchin is gonna die! And it's because of you, you murdering son of a bitch!''

Jeff Dee stood and then fell facedown in the dirt. Two of his gang dragged him over closer to the campfire. For the first time, Slocum got a good look at Helen Frederickson. She was still tied securely to the tree on the other side of the campsite, her eyes wide at the horror of all she witnessed. Slocum wished he could have comforted her.

For all that, he wished she could have comforted him.

He winced as Clement tied a noose around his neck, then pulled the rope taut over a high limb of a larger pine tree. Slocum came up on his toes to keep from choking. With his hands tied behind him he could do nothing to ease the rough hemp slowly choking the life from him.

"That'll hold you. If those spindly legs of yours give out, too bad. You're gonna swing sooner or later. You might just want to rob us of the pleasure of doing it, you lily-livered coyote." Clement laughed and went back to join his companions around the guttering campfire.

The lying and tale-telling continued until, one by one, the gang passed out or fell asleep. Slocum hopped about, trying to see if Helen might work free to save him. He saw only a darkness melting into deeper shadow where she was tied.

He had seen how they'd secured her. He could expect no help from her. And only continued torture from the gang when they sobered up. Slocum tried to shake his head to clear his vision of the matted hair and glass stuck to it over his eyes. Nothing worked. All he accomplished was choking a bit more life from himself.

A fleeting moment passed when he considered doing as Clement had suggested. Rob them of their fun. Kill himself. It would be easy enough. The muscles in his legs had already knotted from the strain of standing on tiptoe to keep from hanging.

Then the cold anger that had been hidden deep inside during the gang's shooting contest surfaced and the embers caught fire. Hot anger filled him. He could die, but he would die with their blood on his hands. Especially that of Jeff Dee.

Slocum funneled his anger toward getting free. He couldn't move, even hopping, to get the rope off the overhead limb. The bark was too rough, and small branches held the rope in place. But there might be another way to freedom. He lifted his hands and felt the knife still sheathed at the small of his back. The gang had taken his rifle and Colt, but had not bothered searching him.

Their sloppiness gave him hope.

Fingers numb from lack of blood flowing for so long, Slocum worked gingerly, getting to the hilt, then the handle. Drawing it carefully, working so he wouldn't drop it, he drew it halfway from its sheath. Then he started rubbing his bonds against the sharp edge. The angle was wrong, and he fought constantly against the fear he would drop the knife.

For what seemed hours, Slocum hung by his neck and worried at the ropes around his wrists. Then his worst fear was realized. The knife slid all the way from its sheath and fell to the ground.

It took Slocum a few seconds to realize he had cut through the tough ropes around his wrists. He hadn't felt them part because the flesh was cold and numb from being bound so long. It didn't matter that he had dropped the knife. He was free.

As quickly as the thrill of success raced through him, he realized he was still in a powerful lot of woe. By dropping the knife he had lost his chance at cutting the rope slowly hanging him.

Loud snores from around the dying campfire assured him they had not posted sentries. He could work without fear of being found out. Rubbing his wrists for several minutes got feeling back into them. But the rope burns around his neck distracted him, and every movement tightened the noose a bit more.

The world was spinning in crazy circles, his blood and air almost shut off, when he reached high above and caught at the rope. Pulling, he took some of the tension off his neck. He had to wait another few seconds for blessed air to gust into his lungs and blood to flow again unrestricted to his brain.

But now what? He couldn't hang like this much longer.

Tugging hard, Slocum found that Clement had secured the rope to the limb above too well. Twisting slightly, he pulled himself higher and took more pressure off his throat. As quickly, he found he could not use just one hand to free himself. His strength faded rapidly, and he could not support his own weight with just the other hand.

Slocum climbed. Slowly, painfully, hand over hand, he climbed until he could kick out with his feet and throw his body belly-down over the tree limb. He didn't know how long he lay doubled over the limb, but he eventually regained his strength and pulled off the noose.

He continued to lie limp, trying to figure out how best to approach the gang.

His overblown schemes were dashed when he heard a loud snort, followed by a belch. One man stirred and stretched. Then came Jeff Dee's loud voice. "You still there, Slocum? Good, glad to hear it." The gang leader laughed drunkenly. " 'Cuz I want you to know I'm gonna sample some of the fine wine you been keepin' all bottled up. Not nice of you. You should share."

Jeff Dee stumbled to his feet, kicked one of his men—who rolled over and grunted something profane—then made his way toward Helen.

Slocum's anger resurfaced and focused entirely on the brother of the man he had killed. Billy Dee had died in a fair fight. Killing Jeff Dee in the same way no longer mattered. Slocum dropped to the ground and landed in a crouch. He fumbled around until he found the knife he had dropped.

A quick slash across the throat from behind would end the outlaw's worthless life. He took a step toward the camp and fell heavily. His legs refused to support him. His calves were knotted from the strain of supporting his body for so long. If he could have willed himself to fly in that instant, he would have.

"Yes, ma'am, you gonna get the finest any man ever gave you," came Jeff Dee's boast. Slocum could see the man's back and how he worked at his jeans. Helen struggled futilely against the ropes holding her, even as Slocum fought to regain control of his own body.

He got his knees under him and lurched forward. He landed on one of the unconscious robbers. Knife in hand, he considered ending the man's life with a single quick slash. That would be one less he would have to kill later.

"You're about the purtiest filly I ever saw. I'll hand it to Slocum. He's got good taste in woman flesh. Lookee here. Never seen a tittie so nice and firm."

Helen struggled to no avail. And Slocum discovered his Colt Navy in the gear dropped beside the outlaw's bedroll. He hefted it, then knew he had better make good sure of the six rounds in its cylinder. The shots would wake all the men—all seven of the sleepers. He could never finish them off fast enough.

He could go from blanket to scattered blanket cutting outlaw throats, but from the sounds coming from Jeff Dee and Helen, he knew he didn't have the time.

Slocum wanted to save her this ultimate indignity if he could. He half crawled and half walked across the campsite. The sleeping outlaws turned and complained at the noise, but no one bothered to open bleary eyes to see who had disturbed them.

Closer and closer Slocum came to Jeff Dee. The man had his jeans down around his ankles. Helen's eyes were wide. Dee had torn her dress, leaving her half naked to the waist. His hands were working on the ropes binding her legs together so he could finish his devilish task.

"You sure are purty," Dee slurred. "So purty, you're gonna love this when a real man shows you how purty you are.'' Dee dropped to his knees and grabbed Helen's legs, pulling her closer to him. She gagged, the scarf holding her neck to the tree not yielding. Dee, in his drunken ardor, never noticed.

Nor did he notice when Slocum buffaloed him with the barrel of his Colt Navy. The loud clunk rang out in the still night and Dee collapsed, his pants down around his knees.

Helen's wild eyes looked up at him, as if he might have been another outlaw come to do her harm.

Slocum slit the ropes binding her, then carefully severed the scarf around her neck. She fell forward, sobbing hard. He pushed her away. Using the tip of his knife, he clipped the string cutting into the sides of her mouth.

''John,'' she gasped. ''It's horrible. I—''

''Not now,'' he said softly. ''I have a horse. We can get back to Last Gasp.''

''Kill them,'' she said harshly. ''Kill every last one of them or I will!''

She grabbed for his gun. He wrestled it away from her.

''I'll do it,'' he promised, but Slocum saw it might not be as easy as he had thought. Jeff Dee rose, pulling at his jeans.

''Gettin' away. The sumbidch's gettin' 'way!'' the outlaw leader slurred.

Slocum aimed his Colt Navy and fired point-blank. Jeff Dee recoiled and fell heavily to the ground. But the gunshot brought the rest of the gang up, every last one of them reaching for his six-shooter.

11

"Run, Helen, run!" Slocum cried. He turned his six-shooter toward the outlaws and opened fire, shooting to make every round count. He heard two yelp in pain, but the response told him he had only winged them. Slocum doubted he'd even slowed them down much.

Worse, his Colt came up empty, and he saw Jeff Dee stirring, groaning, and rubbing his chest. Slocum thought the train robber's hand came away wet with blood, but he wasn't sure. And he didn't have time to finish off the gang's leader. He turned and plunged into the brush after Helen.

Slocum caught up with her within seconds. His arm circled her trim waist and carried her along, urging her to more speed. When they came to the sheer canyon wall, Slocum never broke stride, cutting to his left, going deeper into the canyon. He knew Dee and the others would think he'd tried to escape the Fourth of July Canyon. Slocum hoped to slow them down just enough to gain precious time for Helen and him to recover their strength.

Time. It was all he had—and what he thought he'd run out of. His free hand went to the rope burn around his neck. He owed the Dee gang for this. He owed them a lot more than he had given so far.

"I . . . I can't go on," Helen gasped. Slocum realized she was at the end of her rope. He recoiled slightly when he considered what this meant. If they *didn't* keep going they were both likely to be at the ends of ropes. Jeff Dee had shown he liked that sort of punishment.

"We've got a few minutes," Slocum decided. "They think we'll go the other direction, back toward my horse." He crouched and patted his pockets, hunting for spare ammo. None. His pockets had been filled, but one of the outlaws must have taken it all. Slocum had never noticed. Now his Colt Navy rode empty in his holster.

He drew his knife and checked the edge. Sharp and ready for Jeff Dee's throat.

"That's all?" asked Helen, eyes wide in horror. "All you have to fight with is a knife?"

"No," said Slocum, sliding it back into the sheath. "I've got something better." He tapped the side of his head. "Those are clumsy, stupid men. Dangerous, yes, but they can be outwitted."

He didn't feel very smart right now, after being gulled so easily by Jeff Dee. Slocum had needed a spare gun to help with Helen's rescue, and had not questioned how Jonesy had just happened to be there.

"What are we going to do?" Helen asked. "We're on foot. I can't outrun a man on a horse."

"Why not?" Slocum looked up the steep canyon wall and saw the hint of a path upward. The faint darkness might have been an Indian path, or it might have been made by some cowboy hunting for strays and wanting to get to higher ground for a better look. It hardly mattered who was responsible if it gave Helen and him a way out of the canyon and away from Dee's gang.

"I don't think I can do it."

"Helen, since you arrived at Lamy, you've been

through Hell," he said. "We have another piece of Hell to march through before we can return to Last Gasp."

"And then, John? What then?"

Slocum didn't have an answer for that. He had found the path and spoor showing someone had led a small pack animal up the slope. Possibly a burro or mule. That meant they'd have room enough all the way to the canyon rim.

He started up, stopped a few paces along the trail, turned, and held out his hand to her. She fought an inner battle, then took his hand and let him help her up the rocky path. For an hour they climbed, walking ten minutes, resting five.

"John, I just cannot go on. There's no end in sight," Helen said after the long hike from the canyon floor. She looked down and shuddered.

Slocum looked up and felt the same way. They had covered most of the distance to the rim, but in the dark he had lost the trail. No obvious escape presented itself.

"They haven't found our trail yet. As poor as they are at tracking, they may never find this path," Slocum said.

"I need to rest. Longer, John. Please."

"Here's a small cave. We can get some sleep," he said. The cave was narrow, hardly large enough for the two of them to enter side by side, but it proved to be deep. He could not see more than a few feet into it.

"What if a bear lives here?" Helen asked.

Slocum inhaled deeply, then shook his head. "No scent of bear or cougar. Some small critters might live here, but nothing to worry about."

"Right now, I might wrestle that bear and use it for a mattress," she said, sinking down to the dusty floor. She tipped her head back and closed her eyes. Faint light from the stars outside filtered in, turning her skin to silver and her hair to midnight black. Slocum had never seen a lovelier sight.

He settled beside her and she turned, snuggling closer, her head resting on his chest.

"I never thought it would be so . . ."

"Dangerous?" Slocum suggested.

"Exciting," Helen said. "My life was dull. I worked long hours as a nurse, seeing nothing but dead and dying people. How few the doctors save, John. It is so depressing to watch men and women die and be unable to help."

He had nothing to say to that. He had witnessed too many emergency amputations during the war. Doctors sawed off arms and legs in seconds in a vain attempt to save lives. They lost more than they cured, Slocum reckoned. How that must gnaw at the sensibility of a woman as caring as Helen Frederickson.

"It surprises me you couldn't find a husband back East," he said.

She moved closer, her hand slipping inside his shirt. "I was tainted, John. Imagine. Twenty-eight years old and unmarried. Something must be wrong with me, everyone said. No respectable man would have anything to do with me. I had no dowry, no family connections, nothing."

"I'd say you have plenty to offer any man."

She turned her face up to his. For a moment they stared into one another's eyes. Then they kissed. Hard. Their passion mounted, fueled by the hardship they had shared and the danger they still faced.

Helen's tongue probed Slocum's mouth and rolled about inside it until they both gasped for breath. He broke off, kissing her lips and eyes and ears. He nibbled lightly on her earlobe before working down the side of the lovely woman's neck to her throat. There he burrowed, kissing and wondering if he ought to move even lower.

Helen answered this unspoken question for him. She fumbled at her blouse, letting the torn section fall free and expose one breast. Then she boldly revealed the other to him.

"For you, John. Only for you," she said. Then she sighed in pleasure as his mouth worked over the coppery disks surrounding her nipples and sucked those hard little nubbins of flesh into his mouth, kissing and licking and sucking hard on them. First one, then the other, back and forth. Her breasts became covered with gooseflesh, as much from the cold night air as from the excitement of what he offered her.

Slocum moved lower, parting her torn, disheveled clothing, and finally casting it aside to make a rude bed. Helen helped then, standing to work out of her skirt and frilly undergarments. Slocum felt himself responding powerfully to the sight of the naked woman shimmering in the silver starlight.

"Let me," she said, dropping to her knees in front of him. She worked to get off his gunbelt, then his jeans. Slocum arched his back and let her cast them aside, and soon he was as naked as she.

"How it must hurt hiding that away in tight denim jeans," she teased. She stroked up and down his length, sending tremors of desire pulsating into his loins.

He pulled her to him, kissing harder now. He felt her breasts crush down against his chest. The tiny pebbles cresting each breast felt like a knife thrust. If they were, this was the way he wanted to die.

His hands roved her sleek body, gliding over her back and down to her curving rump. He cupped those half-moons and lifted slightly, getting her into position. Then he reached between them, finding the fleecy triangle nestled between her legs already dewy.

He parted her thighs, letting her straddle him as he lay back on the cave floor. Their clothing provided scant padding under his back, but Slocum hardly noticed. His attention was focused on the woman rising above him, positioning herself, then lowering her hips slowly.

His manhood slipped into her tightness. They both groaned, enjoying the feelings each generated in the other. Slocum reached up and cupped her breasts. Helen sighed, closed her eyes, and tossed back her head.

"I could stay like this all night, John. You fill me so!"

Slocum knew better. She wouldn't be able to remain quiet for long. Already he felt the prodigious pressures of desire rising within him. His iron-hard shaft twitched and bucked in the tight hold of her most intimate recess. He moved a little under her, stirring himself around. This was the trigger that proved to Helen she could not remain quiet any longer.

"Oh, oh," she sobbed out. She put her hands on his chest, lifted her hips, then slowly dropped again. The in-and-out movement was enough to tell her of untapped pleasures awaiting them both.

"Go on, do it now," he said. Using his grip on the twin mounds of flesh as a guide, he lifted her and eased her down a few times. Then Helen began moving on her own, passion wiping out any rational thought in her head.

"Yes, yes," she gasped out, lifting and falling faster now. Friction burned at them, lit the fuse of their desire, and then Helen's hips went berserk. Slocum felt like a human piston moving back and forth in a snug, moist cavity.

Together they moved and strove and aroused until they exploded with all the delight a body could tolerate.

"It's rising like a hot tide," Slocum grated out.

"I'm ready, I'm ready," she sobbed. And she was.

Together they soared away from their woes, past the dangers, and through to a region of mind and body beyond all care.

Helen sank forward, her head beside Slocum's. He turned slowly, rolling her off him. Their quarters in the narrow cave proved cramped, but somehow Slocum wasn't inclined to complain. He held her in his arms until they both fell asleep.

He awoke with a start, hand groping for his six-shooter. He sat bolt upright, and it took him a few seconds to realize his gun was deeper in the cave and wouldn't do him any good even if he had found it. He grabbed his knife and listened hard until he realized what had awakened him was the normal movement of the world outside their cave.

It was less than an hour before sunup, and creatures stirred, hunting for food—and being hunted. The pinched cave mouth opened due east, bringing light inside before it cast down into the canyon below. To his side, Helen still slept. The tension had eased in her face, and she looked at peace.

Slocum tugged and pulled and got his clothing out from under them, dressing quickly. He rubbed his arms to get circulation back. Helen had slept on his right arm all night. More than that, he was cold. The cave had provided some small protection against the cold, but mostly their combined body warmth had kept them from suffering unduly.

Belly growling from lack of food, Slocum went to the cave mouth to see if he might snare something for their breakfast. The dim gray light revealed nothing. A hundred feet below, life began its day in the canyon, but Slocum wasn't going to descend to find food. Their only chance of escaping from Jeff Dee and his gang was to go up, not back.

He wondered if the gang leader had given up the hunt

for them, content he had Slocum's horse. Somehow, Slocum doubted the young man would count this as any victory. He'd tasted blood, he wanted revenge, and he had to outdo his brother in viciousness to satisfy not only his gang but himself.

"John?" came Helen's sleepy voice. "Where are you? It's *cold*!"

"Come on out here and sit in the sun. That will warm you."

He was startled to see her come out right away, still stark naked. She seemed to take a modicum of pleasure at his shock.

"Don't you like what you see? You did last night." She turned in a slow circle so he could see every curve and swell of her lovely, bare body.

"I like what I see," Slocum said, "but we need to find the path and get to the canyon rim. I don't think Dee has given up. When it gets light enough, he might spot us."

"Oh, very well," she said, turning from him. She bent over to sort through her clothing, giving him the sight of her bare, curvy bottom. Slocum had no time for this. Their lives depended on getting to a ranch or finding other help. Still, he cast a sidelong glance at her, feeling his body responding to all she freely offered though he couldn't accept it right then.

After. After they got back to Last Gasp, he told himself.

"Hurry," he called to her. "I think I heard something below." He went past the mouth of the cave to the ledge running outside it. Falling to his belly, he crawled to the edge and looked down. He cursed under his breath. At the bottom of the path stood three of Dee's gang, including Clement.

The man's voice carried all the way up to Slocum.

"I tell you, they took this path. See? See?" Clement

looked up, squinting against the pale light turning the dark sky into vivid blue. "They fooled us last night. Jeff thought they'd try to get to Slocum's horse. Nope, no way, I told 'im. They'll go over the rim. This is it. They went up here."

"You've been eating jimsonweed again, Clement," complained another of the gang. "A rabbit couldn't make it up there. Not even a mountain goat!"

"I'll bring back their scalps," Clement said, resting his rifle in the crook of his left arm as he started the upward climb.

Slocum scuttled back into the cave where Helen had finished dressing. Her blouse still gaped open, exposing her breast now and then no matter how she tied the tatters. This occupied her.

"We have to make a run for it," Slocum said. "Clement and a couple others are on their way up the trail. We took an hour getting here in the dark. It won't take them half that in daylight."

"Can't we stay and fight them off?"

"With what? Roll rocks down on them? They have rifles. They'd potshot me on this narrow trail. We still have some time. If we get to the rim we can get away."

"Do you know where the trail is?"

"Don't know how any man leading a mule got to it, but I see a ledge about ten feet above this cave where it continues. Part of the mountainside might have sheared off, causing the break in the trail."

"If we have to climb the sheer face, won't Clement and the others have a good shot at us?" asked Helen.

"Yes," was all Slocum replied.

He took her hand and led her into the dawn. He pointed silently to the cliff face they had to climb. Here and there jutted hunks of rock to use as holds for hands and feet. It wouldn't be easy or quick traversing those ten feet, but they had to do it before Clement got closer.

As it was, they took the risk of being seen from below. A single shot would bring the rest of the gang running. A few outlaws they might escape. The entire gang would run them down sooner or later.

"I don't know if I can do this, John," she said, licking her lips nervously. "The handholds are so far apart. What if I slip?"

"You're dead," he said harshly. "So don't slip. Go on up, and I'll keep your feet on solid rock."

"All right," she said. Then Helen impulsively kissed him. Spinning, she flattened herself against the rock face and started up, fingers fumbling for the smallest of protuberances to grip.

Slocum waited impatiently as she worked her way up to the continuation of the trail. Her tattered skirts billowed in his face. He reached under her skirts and caught her ankle. In other circumstances, this might be an exciting, arousing thing, but all he could think of was Clement behind—and the chance that Helen might fall a hundred feet to her death on the canyon floor.

He guided her foot to a safe spot, then grabbed her other ankle and set that foot on a still-higher rock. Then he followed, using the same spots. He felt like a fly walking on a wall. The feeling increased, and visions of a swatter crashing onto him heightened when Clement yelled below.

"There they are! We got 'em! The reward Jeff offered's gonna be ours, boys!"

"Hurry," Slocum urged. "They must want us alive or Clement would shoot," he called to Helen. He knew he'd lied. Clement's reason for not firing on them had nothing to do with taking them prisoner again, however much Jeff Dee might want to torture Slocum or rape Helen. It had everything to do with not drawing attention from the rest of the gang and having to share Dee's offered bounty.

"I'm almost there, John. I have a grip. I—"

Helen toppled back, the verge giving way. A cascade of rock and dust showered on Slocum, but he found himself struggling to hang onto Helen, to keep her from plunging to her death. He slammed her hard against the rock face—then felt his footholds beginning to break under their combined weight.

"Climb. Do it," he said urgently. Helen struggled, and got free just as both of Slocum's footholds broke free. He held onto the handholds, and pulled himself up painfully until he found new notches in the rock face that would support him.

"Sideways," he ordered. "Go sideways, then up. We're almost all the way up."

Helen moved slowly, deliberately—and finally rolled onto the trail above. Slocum kept looking down, seeing Clement's progress. He had misjudged how much time it would take the outlaw to close the distance. Slocum and Helen had taken an hour in the dark. Clement and his henchmen wouldn't take fifteen minutes. They were driven as much by a desire for revenge as anything else.

Slocum wished he had killed them all the night before.

"John, take my hand."

He looked up and saw Helen reaching over the edge of the trail. He reached up, her hand circling his wrist. He grabbed her slender wrist, and was surprised at the strength she showed pulling him up.

He sat on the trail beside her, panting harshly. The altitude had gotten to him, as well as the frantic need to keep ahead of Clement. Slocum hated to admit it, but he felt fear gnawing at his guts, as much for Helen's safety as for his own.

"A close one," he said, "but we're not out of this yet. Clement's breathing down our necks." He heaved himself to his feet and started up the trail, seeing it crumbled in places. He wished it would all collapse after he and Helen passed over it.

Nothing of the sort happened.

Gasping for breath, he and Helen reached the top of the trail. The canyon rim extended north onto a rocky patch or south into an area festooned with lodgepole pines.

"If we go north, they will spot us right away," Slocum said, coming to a quick decision.

"South it is," Helen agreed. "But what's south?"

Slocum shook his head. He had no idea what lay ahead. But he found out within minutes when he stood on the brink of a two-hundred-foot drop. Slocum moved even closer and peered down.

"John, what are we going to do?"

Behind them came the loud, jubilant cries of Clement and his henchmen. They had reached the top of the trail and found their quarry's spoor right away.

"There's only one thing to do," Slocum said grimly. He grabbed Helen's hand and jerked her forward.

Their screams as they fell cut through the still morning air.

12

"The damned fools!" cried one of Dee's gang. Rocks rattled over the edge of the cliff and tumbled far below. "Why'd they go kill themselves like that?"

"Yeah," said Clement. "They coulda let us do it for them." Clement went to the cliff and spat. The spittle turned over and over, then got caught by an updraft and seemed to hang for a moment with a life of its own. Then it fell apart and vanished in the dry New Mexico air.

Footsteps clacked against rock and receded. A dozen feet below the lip of the cliff Slocum and Helen huddled. He held her tightly, more to keep her from falling than from the need to comfort her—or himself.

He felt her heart beating like a frightened rabbit's, and she burrowed her face into his chest. Slowly she looked up.

"I thought you were killing us, John," she said in a small voice.

"Wasn't time to explain," he said. He had looked over the cliff and had seen the rocky ledge. It had been pure luck it had held as the pair of them crashed into it. He had scrambled frantically, getting a firm grip on a

119

weed growing out of a crack and hanging on to Helen, keeping her from plunging to her death on the rocks far below.

Now they sat with their backs pressed into the cliff face and tried to calm their nerves.

"Do you think they've left?" she whispered. "I don't know if I can stay here much longer."

She started to look over the edge, but Slocum stopped her. Vertigo would do her in. And holding her if she tumbled would be impossible. He craned his neck and looked above. The rock jutted out, then cut back sharply to where they had jumped. He realized how lucky they had been coming to rest here. Getting back to the top might not be difficult, but would take a few minutes of hair-raising mountaineering.

To stay alive, to bring vengeance to Jeff Dee and his gang, it would be easy as pie for Slocum.

"They need to convince themselves we are gone and then start back down the trail to the canyon. Give them another five minutes." Slocum was worried even this might not be long enough, but Helen needed hope. Five minutes was possible to endure. He would have stayed for a half hour or longer had he been alone.

He held her until she grew restive.

"John, I *have* to get off this perch. Thinking about the drop is driving me crazy." The shrill edge of hysteria in her words convinced Slocum it was time to move.

"All right. You wait, let me go up, and I'll pull you up." Slocum stood, ran his hand along the rocky projection, then began working himself upward. It was easier than he had thought, and he wiggled over the edge of the cliff in a few seconds—to find himself staring down the barrel of Clement's six-shooter.

"Thought you were funnin' me, Slocum. I sent the boys back. Told them I wanted to take a leak. Maybe I should have pissed over the edge of the cliff. You'd a got a real shower then, woulda showed you what I think of a buzzard like you.''

Slocum stood and took a few paces along the side of the cliff. ''You got me fair and square, Clement. What now?''

Slocum was aware of the long drop immediately behind him. Clement turned and followed him, then waggled the gun barrel to stop Slocum's progress away from the verge.

''You stand right there where I can keep you in my sights. If I take you back, Jeff'd give me a big reward. But killing you has a pleasure to it that might be better than money.''

''What's better than money?'' asked Slocum, gauging the distance and knowing he would never reach Clement before a slug ripped him free of his life.

''Revenge. You made me look like a fool.''

''What difference does that make, unless you have ambitions to take the gang away from Dee? He seems a mite young to me. And he's not the cold-blooded killer his brother was.''

''You see that, do you?'' Clement smiled and moved a little closer. Slocum still had no chance to jump him.

''You got the brains,'' Slocum said. ''He's hotheaded, and that will get you all killed eventually.''

Clement started to agree, then whirled around, sixshooter leveled as Helen scrambled over the edge of the cliff. He assessed the situation in a flash, swinging back to keep Slocum covered.

The rock Helen threw crashed into the side of Clement's head, staggering him. Slocum grabbed for the man's gun hand and missed. But Clement was already tumbling over the rim. He screamed all the way down until a loud crash marked the end of his miserable life.

"I killed him," cried Helen, eyes wide and hands flying to her mouth.

"I didn't get his six-shooter," Slocum lamented. He heaved a sigh. At least he didn't have to fight off the other outlaws Clement had brought with him.

Helen went to the edge of the cliff and looked over. Slocum went to her, thinking she might turn giddy. Her words startled him.

"He splattered, as if I had dropped a watermelon," she said, as if fascinated. "He deserved it, didn't he, John?"

"He did. I would have preferred to do it with my own hands, but I'm glad he's gone." Slocum touched the rope burn on his neck. Clement had been brutal, but he was only one of Jeff Dee's minions. The rest of the gang—along with their leader—had to be brought to justice.

"I'm glad I did it," she said, steel in her voice that had not been there before. "He did terrible things to us." With a little sniff, she turned, swirled her skirts, and marched away from the cliff as if nothing had happened. Slocum marveled at the change in the woman. Helen had been a nurse, but had concentrated on saving patients, not killing men who had done her wrong. She'd proved capable of changing the direction of her thoughts and feelings. Slocum thought this just might keep them both alive a while longer.

They hiked along to the head of the trail, where Slocum hesitated. He edged to a spot so he could look down to the canyon floor. He saw the two robbers who had accompanied Clement clattering and sliding to a halt. They had reached the bottom quickly. Slocum wondered how long they would wait for Clement—if they would at all.

Sooner or later, Jeff Dee would demand to know where Clement was. He might send out his gang hunting for him, or he might think Clement had simply moved on. But Slocum didn't think he would. Dee was too clever to believe any of his gang would simply leave without his horse and tack. He would know Clement had been killed.

And he would know who was responsible.

"We've got plenty of time, but there's no reason for us to dawdle," Slocum told Helen. "This time we can go north." He eyed the patch of rock and hoped there was wooded area beyond. His belly grumbled constantly now, and he knew Helen had to be equally as hungry. He wanted to find bushes with berries, edible roots, slow critters who would roast nice and slow over a campfire.

Slocum and Helen stumbled and slipped on the loose rock, but eventually got across the patch and entered a grassier area. Meadows began to dot the terrain, and Slocum realized they were slowly descending. He worried the slope might take them back down into Fourth of July Canyon and Dee's cocked six-guns.

Several times they stopped to nibble at blackberries and other things he spotted, but Slocum found himself increasingly loath to take the time to trap or run down even a rabbit for a meal. He had no idea where Dee was or how the young man had reacted to the loss of yet another of his gunmen.

"I'm worn out, John. I need to stop and rest."

"There's a stream ahead. We can get another drink and then follow it downhill," Slocum said, seeing the water meander down the west slope. He hoped this was as far away from Dee as they could get.

For the moment. When he refitted in Last Gasp, got more ammo, and maybe recruited a few men to ride with him, he would come back and flush Jeff Dee and his murderous band out.

"What are you going to do when we get back to Last Gasp?" Slocum asked her a few minutes later. He lounged back and stared at the white clouds tripping along on a high wind. From the corner of his eye he saw Helen sit up. She dabbed water on a torn cuff and wiped her face with it.

"I don't know, John. I sometimes worked as a book-keeper for the hospital. Perhaps I can find work in this area. I doubt if Dr. Newton requires a nurse. There's not enough people in Last Gasp to warrant it."

"Doubt he needs a nurse," Slocum agreed. He considered her expertise in keeping books. That might be handy for a man like him who had no idea how money came and went. He was more at home managing money during a poker game. If he walked away with a wad, he had a stake for the next few weeks. If he lost it, he had to find other ways of getting money.

For Slocum, having the wealth of Last Gasp flowing into his pocket made him uneasy.

"What's that?" asked Helen, lifting her head up and turning it like a prairie dog hearing a coyote.

Slocum cocked his head to one side and heard a horse whinny. He reached behind him and whipped out his knife. He motioned for Helen to take cover in the thicket beside the stream. Coming to his feet, Slocum turned slowly to pinpoint the direction of the rider.

Climbing a scrub oak, Slocum lay along the bottom limb a few feet off the ground. The thick leaves obscured his vision; they also hid him from the rider moving slowly up the slope. Behind the rider came another and another. Slocum gave up all hope of fighting them off. He only hoped now to stay hidden as they passed by.

The lead horseman reined back and sniffed the air. Slocum tried to catch sight of the man's face, but the angle was wrong and the leaves hid too much. The man dismounted and motioned for his companions to do likewise.

"You can come on out, little lady," came the gravelly command. "I see you hidin' in that bush. It's got to be powerful uncomfortable what with all the thorns."

Slocum dropped to the ground, knife in front of him. He stood and smiled, calling, "It's all right, Helen. This is the federal marshal from Santa Fe."

"Howdy, Slocum," said Marshal Slattery. "We hunted for you. Don't rightly know if we found you or you found us."

Helen pushed clear of the bushes and worked to pick out the thistles dotting her skirt. She finally gave up and joined Slocum.

"Didn't think we'd find you alive," said Slattery. He chuckled and asked, "How many of Dee's gang are we likely to find in one piece?"

"One's dead. Took a wrong step back at a cliff."

"Long Drop? A dangerous place. He must have had rocks in his head," Slattery said.

"He does now, Marshal," Helen said almost primly.

For a moment, Slattery looked confused. When Slocum laughed, the portly man joined in.

"I get your drift," he said. "Who's left in the gang?"

"Winged a couple, but their worthless hides are mostly in one piece."

Slattery nodded. "Better off than I thought. You out of ammunition?"

Slocum nodded. As he did he saw Slattery staring at his neck. Slocum touched the rope burn.

"I've got a big grudge against them, Marshal."

"So I see." He eyed Helen's torn dress and worked on piecing together what must have happened.

"How'd you happen to come this way?" Slocum asked.

"Hunting for you two. Folks in Last Gasp sent a message Dee was kicking up his heels and causing trouble. You were kind enough to bring me one of those road agents, so I figured I might sweep the rest of them up and fill my jail.''

''Who?'' asked Slocum, curious. ''Who sent word to you?''

''Ben Longbaugh. Seems your marshal is stove in and laid up. And a pair of deputies got killed. That caught my attention as much as mention of Miss Frederickson getting kidnapped,'' Slattery added hurriedly. Slocum knew what the marshal meant. The lawman hadn't stirred until he'd heard of dead deputies.

Slattery said nothing for a moment, then continued. ''Why don't you see Miss Frederickson back to Last Gasp, Slocum? And me and the boys will go round up Dee.''

''They're down the other side of the mountain, in the canyon,'' Slocum said. As much as he wanted to level his own six-shooter on the outlaw, he knew he wasn't up to it. His wounds ached, and the new bullet wound oozed blood now and then. He was weak and might make mistakes that could get others killed.

Or himself.

Slocum shook himself, wondering if this was how rich men thought. He had never considered his own safety before when it came to settling a score. And the score with Jeff Dee had mounted up to something higher than the Sandia Mountains.

''You're all tuckered out, and from the looks of you both, you haven't had much to eat,'' Slattery said. ''Take a mule and the two of you can make your way back with no trouble. We got a couple spare mounts with us.'' He turned and bellowed, ''Joe, get your ass moving and free up one of the pack animals.''

''It won't be elegant, but it beats walking,'' Slocum told Helen as she suspiciously eyed the long-eared, can-tankerous mule that was led up.

"We'll pick it up on the way back to Santa Fe—with Dee and his men," Slattery said.

"I wish you luck and wish I could go along. I do want to borrow some ammunition. Riding with an empty six-gun makes me a trifle uneasy."

"I can guess it would," Slattery said.

Less than an hour later, Slocum and Helen set off on the mule, his Colt Navy loaded and a rifle resting in the crook of his arm.

"I know how you wanted to go along with the marshal. Thank you for seeing me back to Last Gasp, John," Helen said. He rode with her in front of him on the mule, one arm around her waist.

"It's a matter of being too banged up to help out," he lied. If he'd had to pull himself along by his fingernails, he would have gone after Jeff Dee. But the marshal wasn't inclined to have one of his deputies ride back with Helen, and Slocum wasn't going to send her on her way alone.

Truth was, he needed time to heal.

As they rode, they talked of this and that, idly reminiscing. The miles vanished under the steady mule, and they rode into Last Gasp toward sunup the next morning. Slocum had ridden in higher style, but never with better company.

"John, there's something wrong," Helen said.

"What? Everything looks fine to me." The buildings were standing and the streets weren't filled with barricades. The threat posed by Jeff Dee's gang wasn't obvious.

Or was it?

"The people," Slocum said, finally understanding what Helen meant. "This time of morning, the streets ought to be crowded with people. Well, not crowded, but there ought to be people everywhere."

"Exactly." Helen slid from the mule, and Slocum

joined her. The mule brayed loudly in way of thanks for getting the load off its back, then set off for a water trough. Slocum let it go.

"The general store's closed," he said. "And the bakery and the bookstore. And where're the people at the feed store?" He scratched his head. He had ridden back into a ghost town.

13

"Did Jeff Dee kidnap everyone in town?" Helen Frederickson asked, her voice small. She peered into the dry-goods store. The shelves had been stripped of merchandise. Rattling the front door showed it was locked. Slocum had no problem putting his boot against it—hard—and knocking the door inward.

They went into the store. Slocum made a quick circuit of the store, noting how some of the goods once on the shelves had been left scattered across the floor. Mostly, it was the cheaper merchandise.

"They left," he said, scowling. "They took what they could and left everything else behind."

"Why?"

Slocum didn't answer the lovely woman. He went back into the street, licked his lips, and wished Last Gasp had a saloon. He needed a strong drink right now. Walking across the street, he went to Mrs. Pond's. She was nowhere to be seen. He cleaned off a pane of glass and peered inside. The furniture remained, but the smaller, lighter items were gone.

Slocum returned to the middle of the main street and looked around. He *had* ridden into a ghost town. Some settlements dried up and blew away slowly, taking months or even years to wither. Last Gasp had taken a shortcut and gone from a bustling, if small, town to one where dust blew endlessly along the street and no one cared.

"Where do we go?" asked Helen.

"Doc Newton wouldn't go, if there's anyone left. And Marshal Dawkins wasn't in any condition to ride."

"They might have taken him out by wagon," Helen pointed out. "Could it be some horrible disease? I saw cholera epidemics that laid an entire city low in nothing flat."

"The water's good here," Slocum said. "Disease would have left some other sign. Dead people littering the streets—or in their beds. Last Gasp is just . . . gone."

He stopped in front of the doctor's surgery, not sure he wanted to go in. The puzzle of where everyone had gone nagged at him like a burr under a saddle blanket, but he was also afraid he might find some terrible answer.

He paused as he thought on that. Was he worried that his wealth had suddenly evaporated like spit on a hot rock in the summer sun? That all that Colonel Marks had given him might be gone? Slocum couldn't decide if that was a problem.

With a quick turn, he opened the door and stepped into the surgery. Slocum didn't know if he was more startled, or Doc Newton was. The doctor looked up from a desk littered with papers.

"Don't you knock anymore, Slocum? Or are you sore in need of fixing up again?" The doc peered at Slocum's arm where he had been wounded again. Slocum realized he must look like walking death. His face and shoulders were cut from the shards from Dee's impromptu target practice, and he needed a bath as much as he did a good night's sleep.

"Where is everyone?" Slocum blurted out. "Helen—Miss Frederickson and I—we just rode in and there's no one to be seen."

"Was there an epidemic?" asked Helen, crowding in past him. Her blouse fell down, exposing her breast. Doc Newton's eyes fixed on it in a decidedly undoctorly fashion. He blinked and forced his attention away from the beguiling sight.

"I reckon there was," Doc Newton said. "An epidemic of stupidity. Rumors spread faster than any plague." The doctor leaned back and rubbed his face with his hands. He fumbled around on the desk and put on a pair of reading glasses.

"Well?" demanded Slocum. "Where'd they go? Why?"

Newton looked up and smiled wryly. "Not all of us believed Jeff Dee and his gang was riding down hard on the town, ready to kill anything that moved. A few of us are left. Marshal Dawkins would have hightailed it, but he can hardly move. He fell out of bed a day or two back and broke another rib." Doc Newton smiled wryly at this.

"They think Dee will kill them if they stay? But Dee is a day's ride to the south!" Helen protested.

"Truth means nothing to a panicky man," Doc Newton said. "I tried to tell them they were safer here than in Santa Fe."

"Marshal Slattery's on Dee's trail," said Slocum. "You sent for him?"

"Ben Longbaugh," said the doctor. "Ben's not gone either. He's sleeping in late, though, last day or two. Why, yesterday he didn't get up until nine a.m. I declare, he is turning slothful. But then there's not much left in the bank. Folks cleaned it out."

"How many are still in town?" asked Slocum.

"A few. More than you might think looking down the

main street." Newton frowned, pushed to his feet, and came closer, peering through his reading glasses at Slocum's injuries. "You need some patching up." He turned to Helen and smiled slightly. "You too, my dear, though you are in much better shape." Doc Newton chuckled as he pointed to the examination table.

Slocum and Helen exchanged glances. Then Slocum shrugged. He had nothing to do other than let the doctor work on him. With the entire town vanished, he again considered riding on. There wasn't anything keeping him here.

"Feels good," Slocum said, settling down into the big galvanized tub filled with suds and hot water. He gasped when Helen poured another bucket of hot water over his head.

"You need any scrubbing?" she asked. "I was a nurse, you know, and I had to give patients baths all the time."

"All the time?" he said, smiling.

Helen dropped beside the tub and rested her chin on the high back edge of the tub. She dropped her hand into the water and idly ran it up and down Slocum's leg. He wondered if she would do anything more. She seemed distracted.

"You look like your head's a hundred miles away," he said. "You reach a decision on going back East?"

"What Last Gasp needs is a reason to live," she said.

"Beg pardon?" Slocum pushed soapy water from his eyes and stared at her. He had seen this look before, usually in prospectors intent on striking it rich, or in compulsive gamblers sure the next turn of the faro card would make them millionaires.

"We need to find a reason for them to return," Helen said, her breath coming faster now. Slocum found himself staring at the same place Doc Newton had, but with less justification. Helen had donned a new, untorn dress, though her nearness prompted Slocum's mind to wander from what the woman was saying so vehemently.

"What did you have in mind?" he finally asked.

"I always noticed, when I worked on the books for the hospital, that people became excited when the *promise* of money was there. We don't have to deliver anything but hope, John."

"I don't understand."

"This is illegal, I am sure, but I read it in a penny dreadful, one of those Ned Buntline stories, I think. What if we placed silver in a mine where there wasn't any?"

"You mean salt a mine?"

"Yes, yes, that's the word. We can salt a mine with silver. I believe you can grind up a silver dollar, load it into a shotgun, and fire it into the walls." She became more agitated as the power of her scheme seized her. She shot to her feet and began to pace back and forth, her skirts swishing damply, the hem wet from the water sloshing out of Slocum's bathtub.

"We couldn't sell a mine like that," Slocum said. "Marshal Slattery would be just as happy running us in as he would Jeff Dee and his gang."

"We don't sell it. That's the beauty of this, John. You already own so many mines. So you salt one of your own and let it out you've discovered silver. This will bring the people flocking back, all wanting to find claims of their own."

"And the merchants would return to sell to the miners," Slocum said. "The question stands. Why bother?"

For a moment, Helen did not answer. She worried at the question like a dog with a bone, then said, "I want this to be my home, John. I am tired of traveling. There is nothing for me anywhere else. I *want* to stay in Last Gasp."

Slocum stood and took the towel Helen handed him. He let the water drip off his naked body, but the woman was too wrapped up in her machinations to notice. Shrugging, he dried off and fetched his clothing. Helen had washed his clothes and they were still damp, but Slocum hardly cared. After a few minutes in the sun he would be dry as a bone.

"We can do it, John. I know it will work. When it is obvious Marshal Slattery has captured the gang, that reason for abandoning Last Gasp will be gone. Then they will hear about your rich silver find." Helen worked avidly, scribbling across a sheet of paper, leaving behind small, precise rows of numbers.

"Aren't you the feeling least bit guilty about fooling people?"

"They left for no good reason. Let them move back for what they think is a good one," she said almost primly. "A town needs a strong hand to keep it running. Otherwise, it will vanish. Look at the other towns up and down the canyon, John. They are struggling. Golden, Madrid, how long will they last?"

"A sight longer than Last Gasp," he decided.

Helen didn't hear him. "We can do it, you and I," she said. "The Black Beauty is a coal mine, but about petered out. That new shaft proved worthless. We can use it. The mine is far enough away so prospectors will have to get outfitted here in town, but not so far away they might get their supplies somewhere else." Helen chewed at her lower lip as she schemed.

Slocum sat down and watched her. He didn't know if he wanted to go along with what had to be illegal—not that that part bothered him. But saving Last Gasp might not be worth the effort.

Then he thought some more about it, about how he had been greeted there and how he had rather enjoyed solving the problems that cropped up. A thriving town made him a rich man. A ghost town left him no worse off than he had been when he rode in with word of the ambush by the Dee gang and a dying Thornton Marks flopped over his horse.

Slocum's mind turned to other things. A slow smile came to his lips. He had considered deeding over Last Gasp to Helen. She was as close to family as Marks had had—or was going to have. He owed it to her to puff up the value of Last Gasp before he moved on. Helen would do well running the town, better than he ever could. Slocum had enjoyed the attention he received, but knew it would wear thin mighty quick.

He went to a cabinet at the side of the room and fumbled inside. He pulled out a shotgun and jacked out a pair of shells. Returning to the chair, he used his knife to open the ends and knock out the buckshot inside. Then Slocum started whittling, using a silver cartwheel instead of a piece of soft pine.

"So we—what are you doing, John?" Helen's eyes widened when she turned to him.

He looked up. "The silver's got to be in small pieces, so it will splatter all over the walls when you fire the shotgun shell. I took out the lead shot. The silver will replace it." He held up a shell.

"Then you'll do it? You think my plan has merit?"

"It'll work," Slocum said. "All we need do is be sure the silver in the mine wall is blasted beyond recognition. It wouldn't do to have a piece showing Lady Liberty poking out of the rock, now would it?"

She laughed joyfully and came to him. Helen knelt, laid her head in his lap, and said, "John, I think I love you."

Slocum hesitated, then went back to loading the shotgun shells with silver.

• • •

It took them the better part of the day to get to the Black Beauty mine. The coal mine was high on a mountain, tailings dribbling from the mouth like black vomit. A pair of shacks at the foot of the hill had provided shelter for the miners and the foreman, but the small shacks had been abandoned for a week or longer. Slocum opened one door and peered in. Field mice scuttled about, seeking shelter against the human intruder.

"They lived here?" asked Helen, shocked. "Why, people in tenements in New York have a better life."

"Paid them well," Slocum said. "Not good enough to keep working, though." He stared up the slope toward the mouth of the mine. He hefted his shotgun, feeling a pang of guilt again. Slocum had to keep telling himself no one was getting rooked. The mine would never be sold on the basis of the salting.

"Should we scatter a few slivers around in the tailings?" she asked, frowning. Helen kicked at some of the black rock that had been dropped along the slope from the mine.

"Don't think that's a good idea," Slocum said. "Miners would have spotted it. Better to find a new stope and salt there. It makes more sense that the vein of silver was only recently exposed." He hefted the shotgun and started up the slope.

Helen slogged up beside him, both of them out of breath by the time they reached the mouth of the mine. Strewn around the mine entrance were miners' candles and a carbide lantern that Slocum could not get to work.

"Candles it is," he said. "Doubt there is any gas in the tunnel, not after only a week or so of being abandoned."

"Pockets of gas might be released," Helen said, as if reciting a lesson. She smiled winningly and explained. "I've been reading the colonel's books on mines and the dangers. Methane is explosive."

"Not much of that in here," Slocum said, finally getting a pair of candles lit. He started into the mine, bending low to get under the strong supporting timbers. Inside he was able to walk almost upright, his six-foot height testing the limit of the mine roof.

"How far does this go?" asked Helen. "As deep as a mile?"

"I doubt it," Slocum said, stepping over the tracks that had once carried cars laden with coal. The rails had started to rust, showing they'd been in place quite a few years. No wonder the Black Beauty was about mined out. Slocum stopped, held the candle up and peered down a drift.

"Here," he said. "There hasn't been any work done down here in months."

"I feel so closed in," Helen said shivering.

"You can go back out and wait," he said. "You don't have to be with me."

"No, John, you don't understand. I *like* the feeling. It makes me feel safe surrounded by so much rock."

This surprised Slocum. He didn't mind being underground, but had never thought of a shaft as being safe. Just the reverse. He had seen too many men die in mines to consider them secure.

At the end of the drift lay rock that had been drilled but never blown. Slocum ran his fingers over the wall and held the candle close.

"Coal petered out about here. They didn't want to waste their dynamite on moving another chunk of rock."

"This the place?" Helen's voice held more than a hint of excitement. He saw the gleam in her eyes and the way her breasts rose and fell as her breathing increased. She was thrilled at their little deception.

"As good as any," Slocum said, breaking open the double-barreled shotgun. "Stick your fingers in your ears. This is going to be noisy." He waited until Helen was turned away, her ears plugged. Then he let fly with both barrels. The recoil sent him back a step into Helen.

Silver gleamed across the face of the wall when he held up the candle again.

"We got ourselves a silver find," he said. Slocum examined a few spots to be sure the silver had melted and smeared just enough to look natural.

"I know, John," she said, stepping between him and the salted wall. She threw her arms around his neck and kissed him hard. He felt her heart hammering as she crushed her breasts against his chest. Her mouth engaged his fully, and he felt himself responding.

"Here?" he asked.

"Yes, John, yes!" she said hotly.

He didn't understand why she hadn't wanted to make love when he'd stepped out of the bathtub, but did now in a salted coal mine. Then all questions vanished from his mind.

She fumbled and dropped his gunbelt. He leaned the shotgun against the wall and reached down, hands circling Helen's ankles. He felt the sleekness of her legs as he moved up slowly. Her flesh trembled under his touch. Then Slocum cupped her buttocks and pulled her closer.

She worked her hands so she could unbutton his Levi's and free his manhood.

"So big," she said in a husky voice.

"So tight," he said, his finger finding the center of her being. Helen stiffened and moaned softly as he ran his finger in and out of her until it slickened with her inner oils. "Want something more here?"

"Yes!"

She lifted her leg and snaked it around his waist. He cupped her buttocks again and rocked back, bringing her up on tiptoe and positioning their bodies just right. Then Slocum lowered her on his steely erection.

Both gasped in pleasure at the feel of him entering her.

Then passion took possession of the woman and refused to let go. She bucked and swung and moved, driving her hips up and down on his fleshy spike. Slocum guided her the best he could. The carnal heat mounted until Slocum felt like a stick of dynamite with a lit miner's fuse.

"Can't take much more," he said. "You're wearing me out too fast!"

"Yes, yes," she gasped, thrashing about. She might not have heard, lost in her own desires. Helen's hips twisted and turned and drove down hard, their crotches grinding together in an erotic fury.

Slocum leaned back and shoved his hips upward in a vain attempt to bury himself deeper. He spilled his seed into her yearning interior just as Helen vented a shriek of pure animal pleasure.

They clung to each other until Helen's leg finally uncurled from around his waist. He let her down gently and stepped back.

She smiled broadly. "You're a winner, John," she said brightly. "And so is the *Silver* Beauty!" Helen turned and rested her hand against the salted wall. Slocum wasn't sure which she had enjoyed more, him or the thrill of doing something illegal.

14

"You shouldn't get your hopes up, Miss Frederickson," said the assayist. He wiped sweat from his face and stuffed the dirty handkerchief into a back pocket. He looked up the slope to the mouth of the Black Beauty—the Silver Beauty, as Helen had taken to calling it. "You tell her, Mr. Slocum."

"I'm afraid Mr. Gunther is right," Slocum said, playing along. "Chances aren't too good silver will show up in a coal mine."

"But it is possible, isn't it, Mr. Gunther?" Helen grinned and tried to keep from breaking out in any more overt display of anticipation. Slocum knew what the assayist from Santa Fe would find. Convincing him it was worth more than a nod and a request for payment so he could get back to Santa Fe and real work was the crux of their deception.

The stolid man grunted, then said, "Rocks might fall from the sky too, but I wouldn't lose sleep worrying over it."

Gunther dropped his gear at the mouth of the mine, worked a few minutes to get a half-dozen miners' candles ready, then said, "You want to show me the find, or you just want me to wander aimlessly in miles of petered-out tunnel?''

''This way, Mr. Gunther,'' Slocum said. He held up a candle, shielding it with his hand until he found a discarded candle holder. Progress was swifter then, with Slocum and Helen leading the way. Gunther followed, grumbling about a waste of time.

Slocum found the drift where they had salted the mine. He turned to direct Gunther down it, but the assayist was nowhere to be seen.

''What happened to him?'' asked Helen.

''There weren't any stopes along the way for him to fall into,'' Slocum said, frowning. He turned, and went a dozen paces back before he ran into Gunther. The man still grumbled, but now it was because he carried a bag of rocks.

''Where else?'' he asked Slocum.

''Down here.''

''I'll be back in a few minutes. Won't take long,'' Gunther said. He vanished into the drift, his footsteps echoing away.

''What's wrong, John?''

''I don't know. He's acting mighty funny.''

''Do you think he—''

Slocum covered her mouth with his hand. Echoes traveled a long way in a deserted mine shaft. He shook his head, then released her.

''Some men have their own way of doing things. No reason to rush him, or point him in any particular direction. He'll find what he finds.''

Still, Slocum worried. He had gone to Santa Fe for Gunther. While there, Slocum had checked the federal marshal's office. Slattery was still on the trail, chasing down Jeff Dee and his gang. The deputy running the office thought the gang had fragmented and run in different directions, but he wasn't sure. Worse, he wasn't sure where Slattery was or what he was up to. Maybe he'd concentrated all his efforts on Dee. But it had been a week and more.

Jeff Dee wasn't *that* good a trailsman.

"John, if we—"

Slocum cautioned her to silence again. Gunther tromped back from the end of the drift. He had his sack slung over his shoulder. This time the sack was even larger.

"You find anything, Mr. Gunther?" Helen asked eagerly.

The man only grunted. When they got out into bright sunlight again, he dropped his bag of rocks and opened his kit. Tiny vials of acids were lined up inside the lid like glass soldiers.

"How long will this take?" Helen asked, as much to Slocum as to Gunther.

"A while," Slocum said. "He's looking for a black sediment."

Gunther worked slowly, methodically, grinding bits of rock to dust, then adding the dust to a small watch glass, where a drop of acid rolled about. The man never hurried, nor did he slow. In ten minutes, he tossed the chemicals onto the ground, closed his kit, and stood.

"You have silver, Mr. Slocum," he said. "Not good ore. It won't assay out more than a few ounces per ton. For gold, that would be good. For silver, all I can say is that it *might* prove profitable for you."

"Might there be a larger vein behind the one you found?" asked Helen.

"In one case, yes. In the other, I doubt it."

Slocum and Helen stood stock-still for a moment. Then Slocum said, "In one case?"

"The site where you found the silver? The one down the drift? Forget that one. Surface smear. Might even have been left by some miner, hoping to gull you into believing something more was there.''

"There is another deposit?"

"Along the main tunnel, not twenty yards down. Just a thin streak, but I was looking for it. Others might have missed it. Thin vein running down and to the left, I'd say. The width of a knife blade here, possibly widening. As I said, Mr. Slocum, this isn't going to make you rich, but it might provide a respectable income, after expenses.''

"Thank you, Mr. Gunther," Slocum said, startled at the news. He had gone along with Helen's scheme to salt the mine—and it hadn't been needed.

"Do you think there might be silver in other shuttered mines along this side of the mountain?" Helen asked.

"Might be. Can't say. Get a good foreman and a couple pickmen. Let them search. That's a sight cheaper than hiring me to prowl about.''

Slocum and Helen watched Gunther make his way down the slope to the shacks where he had hitched his horse. He slung his gear over the horse's rump, mounted, and rode toward Santa Fe, grumbling under his breath as he went.

"Silver, John, there really *was* silver here."

"Don't that beat all," Slocum said.

"I knew it would work, John," Helen said happily.

Slocum rocked back in the chair and stared at the steady stream of people coming into Last Gasp. There had been a few days before the flow started. Slocum figured it took that long for Gunther's find to spark rumors of the biggest silver find in Tijeras Canyon ever. He had expected a few of the people who had left town to return. He had not believed it possible so many folks thought their futures lay in Last Gasp because of a few smears of silver.

"Working too well," Slocum said. "There's not room enough for them. The silver find has turned Last Gasp into a boomtown."

"Glad you see that, John," said Ben Longbaugh, sitting down in the chair next to Slocum. "The money that was taken out of the bank is back—and more. I'm being asked for loans to stake prospectors."

"You giving them the money?" asked Slocum.

"That's what I need to talk to you about, John. Since you own the bank . . ."

Longbaugh's words drifted away as Slocum's thoughts wandered. He owned the bank. He owned the houses and buildings and land under it all. He owned the whole damned town because of Thornton Marks's dying bequest.

Slocum wondered if he had really fulfilled the letter of the bequest. He had tracked down two of the three responsible for killing the colonel, but the third murderer still roamed free with Jeff Dee and the rest of that gang. Slocum had kept contact with the marshal's office in Santa Fe, and Slattery still had not returned from his hunt.

In a way, Slocum had no desire to maintain the fairy tale of silver in the mines, though a foreman had said two men would be working the vein in the Silver Beauty and bringing out enough to pay for the effort.

Most of all, Slocum did not want to deal with requests like the one brought him by Ben Longbaugh. What he knew of banking and risk he could pour into a shot glass.

"So, John, what's it to be?" Longbaugh finally asked.

"Well," Slocum started.

From the other side came Helen's crisp appraisal. "Prospecting is too hazardous a business, Mr. Longbaugh. While it is causing the boom in Last Gasp, your better course is to loan money only for the businessmen willing to bring in stock—and families."

"That's something else," Longbaugh said. "Kids need a schoolhouse. And a schoolhouse needs a schoolmarm."

"Have you considered advertising for someone in the *Las Vegas Optic*?" Helen asked. She went on to detail social conditions that Slocum knew nothing about. All the time she'd spent reading the newspapers and making endless notes in her book had provided her with endless solutions to problems he hardly knew existed.

"The schoolhouse," Helen mused, "can be put in the old warehouse at the far end of town. It's a mite big, I know, but the roof leaks and renovating it for a real storage area is a fool's job."

"We ought to get a full-time deputy too," Longbaugh said. "Dawkins is up and around again, but can't haul off the dead animals. We don't want the likes of that stinking up the whole town. Besides that, it's not sanitary. Doc Newton has been having a litter of kittens over it." Ben Longbaugh pointed to a horse that had keeled over. The owner had stripped off his gear and moved on, not bothering to do anything about the decaying carcass out in the hot sun.

"Perhaps one of the would-be prospectors would work a stint as deputy to get enough for a stake," Helen suggested.

"Good idea. I think one of the men coming to me for a loan actually worked as a sheriff up in Colorado. We can raise the salary a few dollars to entice him. He might end up liking the job better than hunting for silver," said Longbaugh.

Slocum let Helen and Ben settle the details of life in Last Gasp. He preferred to sit and watch it all go by—and wonder what lay beyond the heat haze down the canyon. He was feeling tied down, and the urge to move chewed away at him.

"Mr. Slocum, Mr. Slocum, come quick. The marshal

needs your help!'' A small, thin boy of maybe seven stood in the street looking up at him. "He's got a horse thief cornered and needs help flushing him out. The thief's holed up in the old Zamora place."

"Which is that?" asked Slocum, getting to his feet.

"The adobe down the road from the warehouse we were talking about," said Helen. She had an encyclopedic knowledge of Last Gasp. "You might want to take a rifle. The walls of that house are a couple feet thick."

"Need more 'n that to get the varmint out," Slocum said. "Lead the way, boy." He turned and touched the brim of his hat in Helen's direction. "Excuse me. I got business to tend to."

The man was less of a horse thief than he was a drunk. He had brought a case of whiskey to Last Gasp, hoping to sell it. When he had found no saloon, he'd sampled too much of his own wares and accidentally taken the wrong horse.

In spite of this, Slocum enjoyed the momentary diversion.

On the way back to his chair, four people stopped to ask his advice on running businesses.

15

"Riders coming fast from the south, gonna be here in town a few minutes!" shouted the young boy who had brought Slocum the word from Marshal Dawkins about the drunk in the old Zamora house.

The news spread through Last Gasp like wildfire. Doors closed and windows slammed. Slocum heard rifles being cocked, and even saw a few muzzles poking out of loopholes formed by half-closed shutters. He went into the small, well-appointed office where Helen worked at her endless lists of tasks and grabbed his own Winchester. She looked up from the ledgers, startled.

"John, you made me jump. What's wrong?" She eyed the rifle in his hands. Her hand flew to her throat, then dropped to the desktop and edged toward the top drawer, where she kept a small-caliber revolver Slocum had given her.

"Horsemen coming fast. Might be Jeff Dee and his gang." Slocum considered sending her out the back way to hunt for someplace safe to ride out what might be a lead-filled storm.

"Oh, no!" she cried. "This is terrible."

"We'll take care of them this time. You won't be harmed."

"Me harmed?" She laughed and shook her head. "That's not what worries me. What will this do to those who left Last Gasp before because of the threat Dee posed? They might pack up and leave again if there's any shooting. They jumped like rabbits once, they'll jump higher than the moon now."

"Then we don't need them in Last Gasp," Slocum said hotly. He knew what she said was true, and he didn't care. "Stay inside until the dust settles."

"You want me to fetch Marshal Dawkins?"

"Stay here," Slocum said. The marshal was able to waddle about, but still wasn't up to snuff. His two new deputies, one a drifter Helen had recommended and the other a former deputy from El Paso, would do the real work—if they could be found in time. "Stand clear of the windows, and if lead starts flying, get out the back way. You know that stand of cottonwoods a quarter mile to the east? Hide out there until I come for you."

"I won't leave you, John."

"Just do it," he said, irritated, not sure of the reason for this growing anger at the lovely woman. Slocum stopped a moment, took a deep breath, then said, "You keep that head of yours down, hear?"

"All right, John," she said meekly.

He spun through the door and onto the covered porch in front. He walked to the southern end and sat down, a water barrel nearby should he need to take cover. Slocum rested the rifle against the edge of the porch, then fumbled in his vest pocket for his fixings. He rolled a cigarette, fired up a lucifer, applied it to the end of the cigarette, and took a few soothing puffs before he spotted the roiling dust cloud south of town.

The boy had been right. At least six riders galloped toward town, kicking up a powerful fuss as they came.

He ought to have found Dawkins and the two new deputies. Instead, he finished his smoke, then turned to face the lead rider as he came into view. For a moment, he stood wound tight like a cheap watch, ready to spring in any direction. Then Slocum relaxed when he recognized Marshal Slattery. Sunlight glinted off his badge and the badges of the riders with him.

Slocum ambled out into the street and waited. Slattery spotted him right away and reined back, bringing his horse to a stop a few feet away. The federal marshal stared down at him. He smiled crookedly, as if he had expected Slocum to be there to greet him.

"You're looking hale and hearty, Slocum," the marshal said.

"You're looking tuckered out," Slocum replied. "Come on down. We can find you and your men a dipper of water and something to eat, if you're not in a powerful hurry."

"Hell, man, I need a bottle of whiskey." Slattery looked around. "This hole-in-the-wall town doesn't have a saloon, does it?"

"Doesn't," Slocum agreed, "but I think I can rustle up a bottle or two for you." The drunk outside town had forfeited the remainder of the case of whiskey he had been trying to sell. Dawkins had it. Slocum doubted the marshal would mind sharing it with another lawman and his posse.

"Mighty hospitable of you, Slocum." Slattery dismounted, stretched, and handed the reins to the boy who had brought the warning of approaching riders. Slocum wondered if the boy intended to run the entire town one day. He came close right now.

They went to the porch and sat down, the marshal wringing out the wet bandanna he wore, mopping his face, and only then getting around to the reason he came.

"I've got some news for you, Slocum, and it ain't all good."

"Start with the good," Slocum suggested.

"Me and the boys caught some of the Dee gang. They were milling around like sheep when we swooped down on that canyon, but four got clean away."

"Let me guess which," he said.

"Not Clement, of course. But don't know what happened to him. Went to find his body at the bottom of that cliff and there wasn't anything left but bloody smears. Might have been dragged off and et by a bear."

"The weaselly-faced one and Jeff Dee—those were two you couldn't catch."

"You must have read my mind, Slocum. We got the rest over to the hoosegow in Albuquerque. Circuit judge will be tending to them inside a week. But I feel real bad about losing Jeff Dee and three of his henchmen. He's a lot slipperier than he looks." Marshal Slattery spat. "You got that bottle handy? Dust is sticking in my craw something fierce."

Slocum talked to the boy, who had mysteriously appeared after taking care of the posse's horses. The boy went running off, returning with two bottles in a few minutes.

"You ought to start a saloon of your own, Slocum. Make Last Gasp about perfect. You could run a faro game. Get some frisky little filly to deal the cards and hustle the drinks. You'd pull 'em in all the way up and down the canyon, from Santa Fe to Albuquerque." Slattery pulled the cork with his teeth and took a long drink. He choked, then spat again. "Potent stuff. Tastes like something Long Neck Bateson would try to peddle."

"Reckon that might be the fellow selling this," Slocum said.

"Get him to supply your saloon. Yes, sir, this place

would be perfect,'' Slattery repeated, looking around at the bustle of a boomtown.

"With all the prospectors moving through on the way to the silver find, a saloon might not be out of the question,'' Slocum said. But as he spoke, he wondered if it would be a good thing for Last Gasp. Saloons meant women selling themselves to the miners. He had nothing against this, but the people of Last Gasp had seen fit to avoid gin mills up till now.

Or Thornton Marks had, at least.

Again the responsibility came crashing down on him.

"You're looking morose, Slocum. Here.'' Slattery shoved the bottle in his direction. Slocum took a pull on it, then wiped his lips before passing the bottle back.

"We got to move on soon enough, me and the boys,'' Slattery said. "Thought I had found the trail for them owlhoots, but I was wrong. Jeff Dee's getting cagier.''

"If he wasn't learning to stay low, he'd be buzzard bait by now,'' Slocum said, knowing that at the first chance he would be the one to put the man in a shallow grave.

"I have to get on back to Santa Fe, but I won't let the Dee gang go,'' said Slattery. "I promise you that, Slocum.''

"You've done more than your share already, Marshal. Last Gasp thanks you.''

"Last Gasp thanks me.'' Slattery laughed. "You're sounding more and more like the colonel.'' Slattery got to his feet and waved his posse toward the stables. The horses had been tended and fed and watered. It was time to move on.

Slocum wished he could ride with the marshal. Last Gasp was closing in on him.

Across the street he saw Ben Longbaugh talking to a pair of prospectors dressed in canvas pants and flannel shirts, in spite of the heat. They had come from somewhere colder and farther off to find their fortune in a mine that might yield a few thousand dollars of silver— or maybe not.

Slocum shook his head. Helen was doing a good job running the town. Her schemes for making money were more complicated than anything Slocum could come up with. And she had been pledged to the colonel. She, of all people, deserved to own a share of Last Gasp. Slocum considered what it would take for her and Ben Longbaugh and maybe Doc Newton to be named as his agents. They could profit from running Last Gasp. Might work out for him, if they sent money now and again.

Slocum wasn't sure he wanted to be tied down even that much. Relying on a steady flow of money he did nothing to earn would turn him soft. Starving was no way to go through life, but being fat and sassy with no effort wasn't much better. Living by his wits was part of what kept Slocum moving and interested in finding what lay behind the next rock.

Yes, let Helen have Last Gasp. She seemed to need the anchor, and she was surely better at handling money than he was. It took little enough to keep him happy. She, on the other hand, required a considerable amount. Slocum smiled wryly. Maybe she substituted money for the companionship she had lost with Thornton Marks.

He'd miss her when he moved on.

Slocum had heaved to his feet to go talk with Ben about drawing up the papers when a shot rang out. He turned, looked down the long main street, and saw nothing out of the ordinary. Both of Dawkins's deputies came trotting out of the town jailhouse, hands on their six-guns. They were as uncertain as Slocum.

He shrugged. Just some cowboy blowing off steam. Maybe someone took a potshot at a tin can. As he stepped into the street three more shots rang out. From inside the bank.

Slocum whipped out his Colt Navy, rushed to the front door of the bank, and almost died. A shotgun blast ripped through the wood. Hot buckshot pellets sent splinters flying outward. Slocum staggered and dropped to his knees. The door had been blown half off its hinges.

Inside the bank, Slocum saw two men with bandannas pulled up over their faces as robbers' masks. In spite of their attempt to hide their identities, Slocum knew them.

"Dee!" he shouted. "Come out and fight like a man!"

His answer was another round of double-aught buckshot. Slocum dove to the side, rolled, and brought up his six-shooter, sighting in on the door. The instant one of those robbing varmints stuck his head out, he was dead.

"Mr. Slocum," called a deputy—the one who called himself Cat. He moved good, but not like any surefooted cat. For all Slocum knew, maybe Cat saw in the dark. Right now he wanted someone who could back him up.

"Varela's goin' to fetch the shotgun. We got to keep 'em holed up till he gets back with the shotgun and Marshal Dawkins."

"They have two or three hostages," Slocum said. "I caught sight of at least one customer, and Ben Longbaugh is inside. And he had one or two tellers working." Slocum's mind raced. Jeff Dee might have as many as four or five human shields in there, in addition to the money that had been pouring through the bank.

"What are we going to do? Burn them out?"

"Hate to do that, except as a last chance of flushing them out." Slocum feared fire as much as anyone. In a tinder-dry town like Last Gasp, a spark would spread and take every building with it.

"Dee!" he shouted. "This is between you and me! Get out here!" Slocum shouted.

"Don't hear anything movin' inside, Mr. Slocum," said Cat. "I say rush 'em!"

Slocum considered waiting for Dawkins and Varela and the firepower they provided, then nodded. Time was running out. He got to his feet, dug in his toes, and sprinted for the door. He hit the side of the clapboard building, rebounded, and spun around, six-gun leveled.

"They're gone!" Slocum cried, taking in the entire scene. Two customers lay dead on the floor. Behind the counter where the tellers stood, Slocum saw booted feet sticking out. A teller had been killed.

Cat pressed in beside him, then rushed into the bank to look around. Slocum backed off, considered where Dee might have run, and circled the building. He saw why he had not seen Jeff Dee and his henchmen enter the bank. They had used axes to chop through the back of the building, leaving a hole large enough for a big man to squeeze through.

"They hightailed it out back!" Slocum called.

Cat thrust his head through the hole from inside. "Where'd they go?"

"The stable," Slocum decided. He had a cold feeling in his gut. Jeff Dee had left his horses in the stable to be tended while he robbed the bank. His gang's mounts might have been there the same time as Marshal Slattery's. Crossing paths in this fashion, unknown to the marshal, would amuse Dee.

Slocum took off at a dead run, the deputy trailing and shouting for someone to go fetch Marshal Dawkins and the other deputy. From the corner of his eye Slocum saw the young boy who had been acting as his private messenger take off in the direction of the jail. The cry for help would get to the other lawmen.

Slocum wasn't going to wait.

He rounded the corner of the grain store next to the stable, and almost died again. The shotgun belched foot-long tongues of flame, one from each of the double barrels. Hot buckshot ripped his shirt open and left bloody gouges on his chest. Spinning back, he took a deep breath, then whirled around in a crouch, his six-shooter level and ready to fire.

The door to the stable swung open, caught by the soft warm afternoon wind.

"We got hostages, Slocum. You want us to kill them?"

"I want you, Dee," Slocum called. A figure showed himself in the hayloft. A familiar figure. Slocum fired once at the weaselly-faced man—the last of the trio who had murdered Colonel Marks. Slocum knew the instant he pulled the trigger that he had missed.

"Cat, get around to the rear. Don't let them slip away."

"We got 'em boxed up, Mr. Slocum," the deputy assured him. "No one's gonna get past us!"

Slocum worried about the hostages. Ben Longbaugh had not been among those dead on the floor in the bank. That meant he was held by Jeff Dee. How many others?

"You're not going anywhere, Dee. Give it up. I'll see you get a fair trial."

"A fair trial before they hang me? Or would you consider it fair if you just gunned me down, Slocum?" A pair of bullets winged their way from the depths of the barn.

"Let the hostages go," Slocum shouted, "and it'll be just you and me. You want me dead, Dee. I know it."

"And you want to kill me," the younger man called with a laugh. The outlaw held Slocum off for the moment, but had to know the situation would change swiftly when the marshal and other deputy showed up. Within a few minutes, they could have a ring of rifles pointed into the stable.

But the hostages. That kept worrying away at Slocum.

He dodged and ran a zigzag path toward the door. Two men popped up in the hayloft door and began shooting at him. Slocum felt one bullet strike the side of his boot. He was unhurt, but the force of the bullet knocked his foot from under him. He hit the ground hard. Then the pair opened fire in earnest.

Slocum aimed up and fired, missing both men again, but driving them back for cover behind bales of hay. He scrambled forward, and almost collided with a bank teller walking out with his hands in the air.

"Mr. Slocum, please! He's lettin' me go!" the man called. "He wants you to get back!"

"It's a trick!" Slocum yelled. "Get down!"

The shotgun blared, cutting the man almost in two. The lower part of the teller's body stayed in place, feet planted. The torso twisted slightly, almost entirely chopped free by the blast from the double-barreled shotgun.

"See, Slocum? You got him killed! You ought to do what I say!" Jeff Dee laughed, daring Slocum to charge forward and enter the barn. If Slocum wasn't killed outright, which of the other hostages would die?

He backed off, leaving the mutilated teller lying in the hot afternoon sun. Slocum seethed at the helpless feeling washing over him.

"This is *my* town, dammit," he said to himself. "No two-bit road agent is going to do this and get away with it!"

16

Slocum took a few minutes to reload his six-shooter, seething at how Jeff Dee had him over a barrel. In addition to Ben Longbaugh and possibly a bank patron, the outlaw might have the stable owner and his son as hostages. Slocum had no way of knowing how many the murderous owlhoot held, unless he could worm the information out of Dee.

"Dee!" Slocum shouted. "You have much ammo left? Time's running out for you! Give up!" Slocum hoped to get the outlaw to show himself. A single shot would remove all the danger. The other outlaws, who followed Dee so slavishly, would likely surrender.

Then again, Slocum knew he might have to kill them too. That didn't bother him too much. What they might do to their hostages before he could shoot them rankled, though. He slipped along the wall of a building to the side of the barn, keeping the door in view and trying to figure out some other way into the barn.

Where were Dawkins and that other deputy, Varela?

"I've got enough ammunition to kill these people unless you let us go, Slocum."

"Let you go scot-free without turning out all your

hostages first? You have too much liquor in you, Dee?''

"Don't drink," Dee said with a laugh. "Not since that night when I let the rotgut get in the way of my good sense. Should have plugged you between the eyes, not some damned can on your head!"

"Send out the banker," Slocum called. "As a sign of faith."

"Faith?" Dee laughed again. "The only faith I have is in my own six-gun, not your word."

Slocum knew he'd have to go in before the murdering started. He crouched and started toward the door, moving parallel to the open door. He found the air around him filled with flying lead. Hitting the dusty, horse-manure-strewn ground, Slocum rolled and then reversed directions fast. He got off two quick shots, neither of them hitting anything inside.

Where *was* Marshal Dawkins?

"I'm going to kill you, Slocum." Jeff Dee paused a moment, then added cryptically, "Might be I'll do something worse than perforate your worthless hide. Yeah, I like that notion. I want you to squirm and suffer. You killed Billy, damn your eyes!"

A shriek of pain came from inside. Then a gunshot. Slocum got his feet under him and dashed for the door into the barn. Out of the corner of his eye he saw Marshal Dawkins, Varela, and a dozen citizens coming down the street toward the stable.

They'd arrived too late. Dee was killing his hostages. Slocum had to stop him. Another shot. Another and another and then a volley. It sounded as if a war was being fought inside the barn. A one-sided war with all the killing being done by Dee and his gang.

Slocum popped through the door and moved to his left. In the back of the stable he saw a man. He fired, winging him. This turned the attention of the outlaws toward him. Good. He could defend himself. The hostages couldn't.

At least that was what Slocum thought until enough lead to blow a huge hole in the side of the barn came hurtling toward him. He dropped flat and let the slugs rip past and open a new doorway in the front of the barn. He squeezed off another shot and heard a moan.

"Slocum, stop. They're using us as shields. You just wounded—" Ben Longbaugh's plea was cut short. Slocum thought Dee might have slugged the banker.

"Don't listen to him, Slocum. Go on, shoot at us. I want to hear your lead singing through the air. Come on, damn you, come on!"

"Too late for you to get away, Dee," Slocum shouted. "The marshal's outside with a posse."

"It's true, Jeff. A whole pack of them!" called out the man up in the loft—the one named Henley who had helped murder Thornton Marks.

"Is it now? I guess we'd better surrender then. Go on, Henley. Toss down your gun and surrender. Take the hostages with you."

Slocum suspected a trick. He edged back through the hole conveniently blown open for him by Jeff Dee. He motioned for the marshal and the others to stay back. He didn't know what trick Dee was pulling, but he wanted to be sure no one else got hurt.

"Coming out, Slocum. I got my hands in the air." The skinny one he wanted, the one called Henley, came out amid the hostages. Ben Longbaugh limped, the victim of a stray round. Slocum realized with a sick feeling in his gut that he might have been the one who'd winged the banker in the shootout.

The brief second his attention wandered and he felt a tinge of pity for what he'd done was all it took for Henley to drop his hands, reach behind him, and fumble for a six-shooter.

Slocum stepped up, aimed, and fired. The bullet took the top off Henley's head.

"Get down!" Slocum shouted to Longbaugh and the other hostage, a man in his fifties.

Shots from inside the barn tore through the air. Longbaugh pitched forward into the dirt, shot from behind. The other hostage tried to run rather than taking cover. Slocum fired into the barn, trying to stop Jeff Dee, and found his line of sight obscured.

Worse, his line of fire was blocked by the remaining hostage. The man screamed in agony and grabbed his arm, swung around, and toppled to the ground. This was what Slocum had wanted in the first place. He vaulted over the writhing man, then stumbled when his toe hooked a rock.

"He shot Oakland. Slocum shot Mr. Oakland!" an outraged voice cried from the posse.

"Dee's in the barn! Rush him!" Slocum ordered. He tried to remember how many rounds he had fired. Too many. If only he hadn't wasted a round on the hostage.

"I'm coming for you, Dee. Get ready to die."

"Slocum, stop it!" shouted Marshal Dawkins. "Don't go in there."

"After them. They don't have any more hostages, none left alive," Slocum said. He looked over his shoulder and saw a sight that sent a shiver up his spine. The entire posse had rifles and six-shooters leveled . . . at him.

"Don't go in there, Slocum, or I'll have to order them to shoot."

"I want a piece of his hide," someone in the posse shouted. "He shot Oakland. I saw it with my own eyes. And the other gent. The one he murdered! Slocum's a killer."

"Henley was going for a gun. He had it hidden at the small of his back!" Slocum protested. He looked back into the darkness of the barn, hearing hooves and heavy breathing. A single shot rang out.

This caused a volley from the posse. The only thing that saved Slocum from instant death was the fear and anger flaring in the crowd. They would have missed the side of the barn if they had been locked inside it. But that didn't make the ragged shots from rifles punctuated by the belch of shotguns any less deadly.

"Stop shooting!" cried Slocum, flat on his belly. The sounds inside the barn were drowned out by the angry muttering in the crowd.

"No more shooting, 'less I tell you," bellowed Dawkins.

"Dee is inside. We—"

"Get your hands up, Slocum," the marshal said.

"What?" Slocum was stunned. He had almost gotten his head blown off trying to save the hostages and the marshal was arresting *him*? It didn't make any sense.

"We saw what happened. Henley, you said his name was, came out to surrender and you cut him down where he stood." Varela glared accusingly at Slocum, daring him to deny the allegation.

"He murdered the colonel," Slocum said angrily. "He was the one I promised to bring to justice. And he was going for a hideout gun."

"I didn't see no gun," another in the crowd declared.

Slocum turned, stricken, worrying what had happened inside the stable. "Jeff Dee's in there. He's got a couple more hostages. Maybe the owner and his son. I don't know. *He* robbed the bank, Dee and his men."

"Motive for the killing!" shouted someone else in the crowd. "He's a cold-blooded killer, Slocum is!"

Slocum had the gut feeling the crowd would kill him if he moved a muscle. He stood, Colt at his side, champing at the bit to get after Dee but knowing it wasn't possible. Not yet.

"Roll the son of a bitch over," Slocum snarled. "Check the back of his gunbelt."

Varela rolled Henley over. A silver-plated Smith & Wesson gleamed in the sunlight, tucked into the belt exactly where Slocum had claimed.

"Might be self-defense," the deputy said.

"I saved their lives, dammit!" raged Slocum. "Dee shot Longbaugh from behind. Oakland ran into my line of fire. If I hadn't tried to stop him, Dee or one of his gang would have killed Longbaugh!"

"Don't know about that, Slocum," Dawkins said thoughtfully. "You did cut the man down."

"He was going for a gun, Marshal. He had just killed who knows how many hostages! He would have killed me and you and anyone else he could get into his sights."

"Oakland," Dawkins said stolidly, a bulldog refusing to let loose of a bone. "Got to charge you with shooting him. We all saw it."

"Charge me and be damned," Slocum said. "I want Jeff Dee!" He swung about, aware that Dawkins might put a bullet into his spine. Slocum's anger knew no bounds. He had seen hidebound bureaucrats before, but no one quite as bad as Marshal Dawkins. Lester Oakland ought to thank him for saving his life. A bullet in the arm was a small enough price for getting away from Jeff Dee and his cohorts alive.

The barn was cool and sinister after so much activity a few minutes earlier. Slocum listened hard. Mostly he heard the stir from the posse outside. Dawkins came up, clutching his rifle.

"Where you goin', Slocum?"

"To get Dee. Stay down or he might plug you too." Slocum moved in a crouch, spotting feet sticking out of a stall. The horse in the stall had been shot. So had the stable owner.

"You shoot him too, Slocum?" asked Dawkins.

"Dee or one of his men did it," Slocum said, too furious to argue. Whatever the outlaw did, *he* got blamed for it. This infuriated Slocum and made him double his efforts. He wanted the murdering son of a bitch's blood!

"Another one. Dead," said Dawkins. "This one was shot at close range. His shirt caught fire from the powder."

Slocum held his tongue, moving faster now. He heard nothing in the stable, as if he and Dawkins were the only living creatures. He found another dead body, a woman—a bank customer? Of the stable owner's son he found no trace.

All the horses were gone, taken out through a side door meant for men and not animals.

"They got out that way," Dawkins said. "Sneaked past us, slippery as an eel."

"Quiet," Slocum said. He whirled around, his six-shooter coming up and pointing directly at a tack box. Advancing slowly, he heard furtive movement inside, as if a large mouse had been trapped. Slocum grabbed the lid and threw it back, thrusting his six-gun in front of him. He drew back when he saw the boy inside, cowering. Tears stained his dusty cheeks and his eyes had a wild, lost look in them.

"Are you all right?" Slocum asked, knowing the boy wasn't. He had not been harmed, but he had been through Hell. And that Hell would get worse when he learned his pa had been murdered.

"Mr. Slocum, they shot 'em all down. I saw it. They didn't give any of 'em a chance, not even my dad!" The boy broke down and cried hysterically. Slocum didn't much blame him.

"Reckon that settles how the bodies in the barn got that way," Dawkins said. "We need to get after Dee."

"Something else is bothering me," Slocum said.

"Your other deputy went around to the back of the barn to cut off escape. Why didn't he do anything to slow down Dee's escape?"

"Cat? He's a good man. He wouldn't let them varmints escape." Dawkins didn't sound too sure of himself. He still eyed Slocum suspiciously, as if he might have masterminded the bank robbery and the carnage afterward.

Slocum went to the side door where the gang had escaped. He chanced a quick glance, ducking back fast. He imagined Jeff Dee sitting outside with a rifle sighted in on the door, waiting for anyone damnfool enough to poke his head out. No shot rang out. With a convulsive surge, Slocum bolted through the door and took cover behind a pile of wood.

Keen eyes studied the dry ground, following the tracks of the horses. Slocum tried to figure how many men Dee had with him. Slim Henley was dead. Did that leave the gang leader with only two henchmen?

Henley certainly had not been the best of the ragtag gang. Anyone still riding with Dee had to be more dangerous. The little weasel of a man had probably not been the one to actually shoot the colonel. But all three of the attackers from so long ago were dead.

Slocum's only problem was gathering new names to eliminate. Jeff Dee's was at the top of the list.

"Rode off, they did. See the marks in the dust?" asked Dawkins.

Slocum saw the evidence and had moved past to discover why Cat had not put up a fight to stop Dee from escaping. It might have been a lucky shot, or it could have been the result of good marksmanship. Whichever it was, a single round had caught Cat in the chest. From the surprised look on the deputy's face, he might have died before he hit the ground.

"Dang," grumbled Dawkins. "It's gonna be harder

than ever getting another deputy. This makes three I've lost in the past month.''

Something more than recruiting lawmen worried Slocum. He thought back to the taunts Dee had so easily tossed out.

''He had something in mind when he left,'' Slocum said slowly. ''Something to get at me, to make me suffer.''

Shock hit Slocum like a sledgehammer.

''Helen!'' he gasped.

17

"Marshal, have you seen Miss Frederickson?" Slocum asked.

"Hell, no, I been makin' my way over here to clean up after the massacre," the marshal said. "*Your* massacre, Slocum."

Slocum took the time to reload his six-shooter, grabbed a fallen rifle, and set off at a run. Some in the posse shouted after him—and the words weren't encouragement. Slocum felt the tide turning against him in the town he had kept alive.

Fuming, he realized no one except Helen knew what he had done to keep these people's homes intact. Salting the old coal mine had been a crazy idea, but it had worked out just fine. He could still hardly believe there had been a real silver vein waiting to be found amid the tons of black carbon.

He had brought the people back, he had brought all three of Colonel Marks's killers to six-gun justice, he had done more than his share to eliminate the threat posed by Jeff Dee and his gang, and now all they could think of was a chance shot that had wounded one of the town's citizens.

Slocum had warned Oakland to drop and stay clear of the shooting. The man was lucky he hadn't had his head blown off like too many of Jeff Dee's other hostages. Slocum shuddered, thinking of the teller cut in half by the shotgun blast from behind. None of the posse had seen that murder. All they'd concentrated on was a single random shot.

Slocum skidded to a halt in front of the office where Helen had been working. He levered a round into the rifle's firing chamber, then used the barrel to poke open the door. It creaked slightly. Unlike so much of the colonel's old empire, this building had not been kept in tiptop condition. The screech of metal grating on a metal hinge set his nerves on edge.

He spun around, rifle ready to fire. The room was empty.

Slocum stood stock-still, every sense straining. He heard nothing. He ran everything Dee had said over and over in his mind. The outlaw had hit upon a scheme to torture Slocum. What else but to kidnap Helen and kill her—after doing unspeakable things to her?

"I told her to head for the clump of trees out back," Slocum said to himself, remembering his orders to the lovely woman. She had not seemed inclined to obey, but Slocum clung to this faint thread of hope. He went to the rear door and eased it open, peering out.

He went cold inside when he saw how the grass immediately behind the office had been cut up by horses' hooves. Dee's entire gang had ridden here. It had to be them. The rest of Last Gasp had been focused on the stable and the gunplay there.

"He sneaked out after killing Cat," Slocum guessed. "He rode straight here and took Helen." Going out back, Slocum dropped to one knee and ran his finger over the hoofprints cut deep into the ground. Water had leaked from a barrel and turned part of the ground to mud. The prints were as clear as if they had been carved into stone.

Slocum hefted the rifle and headed in the direction taken by the riders. After only a hundred yards he'd seen nothing to tell him Helen had been taken. But his gut feeling was that she had. It fit everything Jeff Dee would think and do.

He turned and went back to the office, opened the desk drawers, and found the six-shooter in the top drawer. Helen had not taken it with her. Had she merely gone down the street with the rest of the crowd to watch the gunplay? Or had she been kidnapped again?

Slocum started for the door, but bumped into Marshal Dawkins.

"Thought I might find you pokin' around here, Slocum. The doc wants to see you. It's about Ben Longbaugh."

"Is he going to make it?"

"Don't know. But I do know I don't want you leavin' town till we decide what to do."

"About what?" asked Slocum.

"You shot Lester Oakland. He's madder than a wet hen and gettin' madder. And there's some question about what happened in that shootout. How'd Cat get hisself killed?"

"Jeff Dee and his gang," Slocum said slowly, "got out the side of the stable. They shot Cat to do it."

"You were in the front. How come you didn't know it was happening? You just let them shoot down my deputy?"

"Where were you and Varela? Took you way too long getting to where the action was," Slocum said angrily. He regretted the implied cowardice the instant he said it. Dawkins wasn't a man for handling real lawbreakers. He kept the streets clear of dead animals and greeted people well enough, but when it came to facing killers, he left something to be desired.

"I ought to lock you up and . . ." Dawkins let his sentence trail off when he saw the thunderclouds of anger forming on Slocum's face.

"I want a posse, ten men or better willing to stay out a week or longer if necessary," Slocum said angrily. "I think Dee has kidnapped Miss Frederickson again. This time I want to make sure he doesn't have a chance to harm her. That means we have to ride hard and overtake him before he feels safe."

"Can't do that. The townspeople would lynch me if I let you leave town. And how do you know Miss Frederickson has been taken?"

"Ask around town. See if anyone's seen her since the gunfight at the stable."

"You're in no position to give orders, Slocum. Get on over to Doc Newton's. I'll see you there."

"You will ask about Helen?"

"Yeah," Dawkins said, but Slocum wasn't sure if the marshal meant it. The lawman turned and stalked off, grumbling to himself. Dawkins stopped in the middle of the street, pointed back in Slocum's direction, then down toward the stable, questioning the cowboy he collared. The cowboy shook his head and backed off, wanting nothing to do with Dawkins.

Slocum let the marshal continue his hunt for Helen. As he hurried to the doctor's surgery, he asked after Helen. Everyone gave him the same answer—those who would talk to him. Slocum got the idea he had become an outcast in jig time. He pushed into Dr. Newton's office and hesitated.

"Come on in. Don't let all the flies in. I do what I can to kill the ones who do make it inside out of the sun, but they get ahead of me." Doc Newton sat at his desk, peering at a book over the tops of his reading glasses, as if this might change what he saw.

"Dawkins told me you wanted to see me. Is it bad news?"

"What? About Ben? It's not good, but I think he'll make it. I'm a durned good doctor, you know." Newton closed the book and leaned back, looking older than his years. "Sometimes, though, I just want to go fishing and never come back. You have those days, son?"

"Mine are getting closer all the time," Slocum said.

"Can't figure people. You try to save the hostages, Ben included, and the townspeople turn on you." Doc Newton dropped his glasses on the desk and rubbed his face. "Go on in and see if Ben's awake. He wanted to talk with you."

Slocum went to the other room, pushed aside a curtain, and looked in. Ben Longbaugh lay on the bed, white as paste and eyes dark, sunken pits. The banker was alert, though, and motioned weakly for Slocum to enter.

"You look like death warmed over," Slocum said.

"You have a way with sugarcoating everything, don't you, Slocum?" Longbaugh laughed, then coughed. "I want to thank you for saving me back there. Dee would have cut us all down like a sheaf of wheat. Don't care what that fool Les Oakland says. You saved us."

"You heard about that?"

"I'm shot, not dead," Ben said. He coughed again. "The doc thinks he's got me patched up all right. I'll be fit as a fiddle in a few weeks."

"The town needs you. A boomtown can't have enough loans being passed out by the banker."

Longbaugh smiled. Then the smile faded. "I know what you want me to do with the land deeds. If you make Helen your agent, that ought to satisfy everyone concerned, including the law."

"See to it when you are able," Slocum said. He sucked on his teeth a moment.

"What's the matter, John? I can read you like a book. I'm not going to die. Too ornery for that."

"It's Helen. I think Dee and his gang have her again."

"Go fetch her back, man! How can I do up all these legal documents if you don't know where she is? Do I have to tell you everything! Go on, git!"

Slocum almost laughed at the banker's attitude. Men like Ben Longbaugh were rare.

He stopped in front of Doc Newton's desk. The doctor studied the book again. Slocum saw it was an anatomy book.

"He *is* going to make it?" Slocum demanded.

"There's some damage inside I'm not too sure about. Might have to operate to patch him up all the way. But he'll make it. He's a young man. Well, younger than I am, so that makes him a young'n to me. And I heard what he told you, Slocum. Go fetch that purty little girl back here."

"Dawkins is asking around town to see if she's around."

"You don't think so. Neither do I. And what difference does it make? You want to bring Jeff Dee and his cutthroats to justice, whether they have Helen or not. So vamoose. Shoo. Get out of here, and don't let in any more flies. Hate the damn things," Doc Newton groused.

Down the street Dawkins had assembled a half-dozen men. From their angry grumbling, Slocum doubted the marshal was asking about Helen. If he stayed any longer he would find himself thrown in jail. Depending on how much Oakland roused the rabble, Slocum thought he might have a rope around his neck.

His hand went to the raw burn left there by Jeff Dee's

noose. Slocum had no complaint with the people of Last
Gasp. He did with the outlaw. Long strides took him
toward the stable. Slocum found his horse outside, standing in the shade. Poking around a bit, he found some
spare ammunition, stuffed it into the saddlebags, then
mounted. Leaving Last Gasp this time was a relief.

Slocum circled the town, picked up the gang's trail
where he had left it while on foot, and rode for fifteen
minutes until he came to a small stream. Dee thought he
was playing it cagey having his men ride into the stream.
It took Slocum less than a minute to figure which direction they'd traveled. The mud was riled upstream but
not down.

He kept his horse moving along at a fast walk until
he picked up the trail again that Dee and his henchmen
had left and headed due west toward the meandering
canyons interlacing the Sandia Mountains.

Slocum urged his horse to an even faster gait. Time
pressed down hard on his shoulders now. Every second
he failed to put a bullet into Jeff Dee's head meant more
danger for Helen. As he rode, Slocum wondered at his
own motives. She had been pledged to Colonel Marks.
Was it only her courage he admired? She was smart as
a whip and ran the day-to-day business of Last Gasp
better than the colonel had, from all accounts.

She deserved the land under the town as her dowry
for a marriage never performed or consummated.

But Slocum knew it was more. Helen Frederickson
had courage and beauty, and too seldom had he found
a woman as appealing. He had wrapped her up in the
web of trouble spun by Jeff Dee and owed her some
modicum of safety.

He told himself these were the reasons he kept on
Dee's trail, but he knew it was also personal between
him and the outlaw. No man did to him what Dee had

done and lived. Before the day was over, one of them would be dead.

Slocum didn't intend to be buzzard bait any time soon.

The day was dying when Slocum began to despair of overtaking Dee. The only consolation he saw in the outlaw's rapid departure from Last Gasp was the lack of time it gave him for any devilment when it came to Helen. Slocum thought he knew the man's intentions. He would go to earth and then get his full brutal pleasure from raping and torturing her.

Slocum turned into a canyon, barely able to follow the trail in the gathering twilight. He wondered if he ought to keep on in spite of the dark, or if he dared stop for the night, when he heard a loud shriek of agony echoing down the canyon.

"Helen!"

His hand flashed for his six-shooter, but the cry had come from some distance. Slocum dismounted, grabbed his rifle, and went forward on foot, knowing it might take longer this way but wouldn't alert Dee or any sentries he'd posted.

Slocum was going to wipe out the entire den of vipers this time. Every last one of them.

18

There had to be at least three of them, Slocum figured.
Marshal Slattery had told him that four had gotten away,
including Jeff Dee. One had died in Last Gasp after the
bank robbery.

But Slocum had to be sure. He decided he would re-
connoiter, then go straight in, guns blazing.

Then good sense shook him free of the wild, romantic
notion of a blazing six-shooter saving Helen Frederickson. If anything, such an attack would guarantee her
death. Jeff Dee had no compunction against killing a
woman if it brought him a measure of revenge. Hatred
burned like a forest fire in that one.

Slocum had to remember it. And use it.

Moving slower now that the dark had descended and
cloaked the ground, he tried not to step on too many
dried leaves or twigs. He had snuck up on an enemy
camp better before, but no one was giving him a reward
for doing it nice. He just wanted it done.

Almost immediately he spotted one sentry silhouetted
against the evening sky. The man sat like a vulture
perched on a high rock. Slocum guessed he had a view
of the trail leading into the gang's camp, but like so

many in this gang, he didn't know squat about staying alive.

Slocum proved that in a hurry. Laying down his rifle and putting the keeper on the hammer of his Colt, he drew his knife, circled the rock where the man stood guard, then silently crept up the back like a spider advancing on a fly.

Slocum was as silent as a night breeze, but something gave him away at the last instant. The man half turned, spotted him, and started to call out. Slocum launched himself forward, his knife tip in the forefront. The blade caught the man under the chin and drove straight up through his mouth and into his brain. He died instantly.

And that proved to be Slocum's undoing.

The outlaw's rifle fell from limp fingers, rattled across the rock, and slid into the night to smash against the ground. The sharp report as the rifle discharged startled even Slocum, who had expected it.

"O'Riley!" came the shout from deeper in the canyon. "You see something, O'Riley?"

O'Riley was never going to answer, not ever again. Slocum pulled the blade out of the man's throat and wiped it on the convenient shirtfront.

"We got company!" came the cry.

"No, wait, gun slipped from my fingers. Fell asleep," Slocum called, hoping to buy himself—and Helen—a few minutes of confusion.

"O'Riley? That you? You sound funny."

Slocum homed in on the yammering man. His voice was like a lighthouse in a foggy night. Slocum hit the ground and started circling, thinking to approach the man from the flank. The tactic didn't work. The man knew his friend was gone and had laid a trap for Slocum.

The instant Slocum stepped from behind a pine he knew he was in a world of trouble. The cocking sound of a six-gun was as loud as the opening of a hangman's trapdoor on a gallows. Slocum pitched forward and felt the bullet tear through his flesh. The slug hit him on the right side, just above his gunbelt. He took a few seconds to examine the wound.

The lead had passed through him, cutting a hole less than an inch in from his side. Slocum moved and winced at the pain, but didn't feel anything important inside him protest the movement. He found some dried leaves and pressed them against the freely bleeding wound until they caked and stuck. The flow was stanched. For a few minutes.

"I hit him, I hit him!" came the cry.

"Be careful," warned another gang member. Slocum strained to hear Jeff Dee's voice. Neither of these outlaws was the one he truly wanted. Lying still in the pile of leaves around him afforded Slocum the chance to study the stand of trees. He had blundered out into a clearing, making a perfect target for the waiting outlaw.

He wouldn't make that mistake again.

Slocum slid the leather thong off his six-shooter and drew the weapon. Twinges of pain shot into his right side, but he ignored them. He had to.

"Where's the body? You know Jeff wants to see the body 'fore he believes you done kilt Slocum."

Slocum got a fix on the second man. The two of them foolishly stood near one another. He bided his time, hoping his wound wouldn't open and start bleeding again. That would weaken him when he needed his strength the most.

"Good things come to him who waits," Slocum muttered. The two men were as foolishly in a hurry as he had been. They stomped and tramped in a straight line for him. He lay on his belly in the dark, waiting for the right instant.

It came with the unexpected suddenness of lightning in the twilight.

They reared up, presenting Slocum with perfect targets. Four times he fired. The first man he hit three times, sending him to the Promised Land. The other spun about, cursing. He had been winged in the gun hand. Slocum saw the man's six-shooter drop to the ground.

Slocum reared up and fired his last two shots at the fleeing outlaw. Scooping up the man's fallen six-shooter, Slocum sent six more slugs flying after him. Then he tossed aside the outlaw's empty pistol and hefted the dead man's rifle.

He had hunting to do. And still there was no sign of Jeff Dee or his captive.

Slocum almost fell over the third outlaw's body. He had winged him in the hand, all right. Then the bullet had kept on flying and buried itself in the man's belly. He moaned and thrashed about weakly, turning to look up at Slocum.

"Hurt bad," he said. "I'm dyin'. You killed me!"

"No," said Slocum. "Not then. Not back there. Now." He leveled the rifle and fired a single shot that put the man out of his misery. As badly hurt as the outlaw had been, this was a mercy. Slocum would do it for a horse with a broken leg. There was no reason not to be as kind toward human debris.

Slocum's own wound began to throb. He took the time to rip off the dead outlaw's shirt and use it as a bandage to hold a wad of cloth against both the entry and exit wound. Already having wasted a considerable amount of time, Slocum decided reloading wouldn't take much longer. He fumbled a great deal, and his fingers turned nerveless now and then from the pain he felt, but he finished reloading his Colt Navy and picked up the rifle he had taken.

Three down. Were there any more in addition to Dee? Slocum trooped along, every sense straining. He didn't see or hear anyone else. Instead, his keen sense of smell caught a whiff of Helen's perfume. Turning, he found the direction of the wind. Dee had grown careless, staying upwind like this. Or was it another trap?

Slocum decided there was nothing subtle about Jeff Dee. This might be a trap. More likely, he had grown careless, or had never thought Slocum was skilled enough to detect the faint aroma.

Slocum headed directly into the wind, his nose working like a prairie dog's. A dozen yards into the stand of trees he spotted Helen tied to a white-barked aspen. She fought against her bonds and had a gag in her mouth. Bait in a trap. Slocum tried to figure where Jeff Dee might be and couldn't.

Making a beeline for Helen, he dropped behind the tree and severed the ropes around her wrists.

"Don't make a sound. I know he's here somewhere."

She made muffled sounds through the gag. Slocum pulled the gag from her mouth, and she gasped the cold mountain air in deeply. Before she could speak, Slocum clamped his hand over her mouth.

"Is Dee alone? Nod if he is." She did.

"Do you know where he is? Nod if you do." Her head remained still. He released her and said, "Stay here until I find him. Then clear out fast."

"No, John!"

"Do it," he said. "Even better, give me a few minutes, then clear out. That might flush him so I can take him."

"Kill the son of a bitch!" she snarled.

"Has he hurt you?"

"He told me what he would do after he caught you. He's an animal, John. Not fit to live. Kill him for me!"

For a moment, Slocum stayed frozen. Then he moved away and went hunting. He doubted Dee hid behind any of the spindly-trunked trees in this copse. He would reveal himself far too easily.

The hooting of an owl caused Slocum to react fast. His rifle came up, pointing into the high tree limbs. He relaxed when he realized it was just an owl giving vent to a mating call. But the wise old owl had warned him where Dee hid. In the thicker limbs, up high where he could get a good shot . . . as Slocum crossed a patch of debris-free land immediately in front of where Helen had been tied.

As if on cue, Helen made a great rustling and rattling as she crashed through the underbrush in her escape. Above him leaves rustled in an oak tree. Slocum fired without seeing his target. Jeff Dee let out a yelp and returned fire. Slocum began methodically firing, boxing in one area on the branch with every shot, wanting to be certain Dee didn't escape into the night.

His heavy, accurate rifle fire cut through the branch. It came crashing to the forest floor, Jeff Dee clinging to it for dear life. The impact momentarily stunned the outlaw. When he recovered he stared down the bore of Slocum's rifle.

"Nice evening to go bird watching," Slocum said. "You ought not fall out of the trees. Scares the little critters in the forest."

"You—" Jeff Dee got no farther. Slocum swung the butt of his rifle and caught the man under the chin. The outlaw's head snapped back, sending him to the ground, arms outthrust and completely unconscious.

"Kill him, John. Shoot him," came Helen's cold order. "He was going to rape me, then sell me into slavery. He said he knew some Mexican slavers who would take me into central Mexico. He's an animal. Shoot him."

Slocum felt tired, completely drained of all emotion. He had killed three men already tonight. What was a fourth, when it was Jeff Dee? The man was a train robber, a killer, a kidnapper, a would-be rapist. He deserved no consideration.

Slocum's finger tightened on the trigger, then relaxed.

"I want him to stand trial," Slocum said. "That'd be worse than anything I can do to him. Death is too good."

"Mr. Slocum, Mr. Slocum," came the telegrapher's shrill call. Pond hurried from the Western Union office waving a flimsy yellow telegram. "They convicted him. They're gonna make him swing!"

Slocum sat on the porch in front of the office. Helen was inside making everything run smoothly in Last Gasp. Ben Longbaugh hobbled about with a cane across the street, healing and soon to be whole.

"What's that, John?" Helen asked. She came from inside. He saw her face and thought anew how lovely she was. Ben had drawn up the papers a week back, as soon as he was able, and had appointed Helen Slocum's agent. Some of the land and businesses Slocum had given to the proprietors. It gave them reason to stay in Last Gasp and not move on at the first sign of the silver mine petering out.

He shook his head. The vein the assayist had discovered did not peter out. It had widened. Prospectors poured into Last Gasp every day now, needing goods and maps of the area. Slocum had arranged it so Helen got whatever profits there might be from the businesses he still owned as her due for all the hard work.

For his part, Slocum was happy with the thick wad of greenbacks riding in his jacket pocket. He was rich enough. His gaze shifted from the excited telegrapher to the far end of town. Last Gasp had grown in the three weeks since he had brought Jeff Dee back and seen the outlaw put into Marshal Dawkins's jail.

A few days after that Slattery had come for the gang leader. And all the while the town had been abuzz about Helen's daring rescue—and how Slocum could have killed Dee and had not. The wind had gone out of Lester Oakland's sails. Townspeople remembered the shootout at the stable more the way it happened, or so it seemed to Slocum.

He was a hero again—and he had divested himself of responsibility for running the town.

"Miss Frederickson, Mr. Slocum, the jury brung back a guilty verdict on more murder counts than you can shake a stick at. They're gonna swing Jeff Dee at the territorial prison next week."

"He deserved to suffer more," she said. She put her hand on Slocum's shoulder and squeezed gently. "But I *am* glad you did not kill him when you had the chance. You can kill when you have to, John, but you're not a murderer. Not like Dee."

"Miss Frederickson!" called the new owner of the general store. "Do you know anything about the shipment of tenpenny nails? It was supposed to reach Lamy last week."

She smiled and shrugged at Slocum, telling him duty called.

"Go on," Slocum told her.

She and the store owner went into the office. Slocum took the telegram from Pond and read it twice, just to be sure. Then he folded it and stuck it into his shirt pocket.

"Everything going all right now, Slocum?" asked Ben Longbaugh, hobbling over and sinking down on the boardwalk beside him.

"Just fine," Slocum answered. A long silence settled, interrupted only by the rattle of wagons or the clank of chains and the neighing of draft horses.

"What are you going to do?" asked the banker.

"Go for a ride, Ben. I'm going for a ride."

"A long one?"

Slocum shrugged. He wasn't much for staying in one place too long, and Last Gasp had come to feel more like a prison than a home. He shook Longbaugh's hand, then headed for the stable. The young man who ran it now was a cousin to the stable owner who had been killed. Slocum had given him the business in exchange for the promise the stable would be turned over to the dead man's son when he came of age, if he wanted to continue on in the family business.

"All saddled and ready to go, Mr. Slocum," said the boy. "You get 'er back by sundown and I promise I'll curry 'er real good."

"Thanks." Slocum flipped the boy a silver dollar. It spun in the bright New Mexico sun, then vanished as the boy neatly captured it.

"Thank *you*."

Slocum mounted and looked back down the street. Ben still sat on the steps of the office where Helen worked to keep the gears of commerce greased with her expertise. He ought to stop off and say good-bye.

He turned and rode to the north, out of town, not hurrying but not dawdling either. An hour's ride brought him to a high rise. He saw Santa Fe to the north, nestled at the base of the Sangre de Cristo Mountains. And to the south lay Last Gasp, newly prosperous—and run by the smartest, loveliest, most attractive woman he had ever found. For almost ten minutes he sat astride his horse and thought hard.

North to Santa Fe and the endless horizon beyond? Or back to Last Gasp?

Slocum made his decision. He smiled with a passing pang of regret, but knew he was right and put his spurs to his horse's flanks.

J. R. ROBERTS
THE
GUNSMITH

LONGARM

Explore the exciting Old West with one of the men who made it wild!